"You Kidnapped The Wrong Girl."

Shane Nichols looked incredulous. "What did you say...what do you mean, *the wrong girl?*" Did she think he was going to take her back in all the snow and trade her in on someone else if she denied her identity? "And I wasn't *kidnapping* anyone!"

"Excuse me. Commandeering."

Shane nodded, justified.

But then she shook her head and gave him a pitying look. "So, consider me commandeered. But I can't change who I am. And I'm Poppy. Not Milly. It was...really sort of noble of you," Poppy added, recognizing his attempt to help out his friend.

Noble, right! Thanks to his age, his thumb and the doc's orders, Shane had managed to make a complete and utter fool of himself at age thirty-two, stone-cold sober.

He'd taken the wrong girl.

And, worse, all he wanted now was to seduce her!

Dear Reader,

Hello! For the past few months I'm sure you've noticed the new (but probably familiar) name at the bottom of this letter. I was previously the senior editor of the Silhouette Romance line, and now, as senior editor of Silhouette Desire, I'm thrilled to bring you six sensuous, deeply emotional Silhouette Desire novels every month by some of the bestselling—and most beloved—authors in the genre.

January begins with *The Cowboy Steals a Lady*, January's MAN OF THE MONTH title and the latest book in bestselling author Anne McAllister's CODE OF THE WEST series. You should see the look on Shane Nichols's handsome face when he realizes he's stolen the wrong woman...especially when she doesn't mind being stolen or trapped with Mr. January one bit....

Wife for a Night by Carol Grace is a sexy tale of a woman who'd been too young for her handsome groom-to-be years ago, but is all grown up now.... And in Raye Morgan's *The Hand-Picked Bride*, what's a man to do when he craves the lady he'd hand-picked to be his brother's bride?

Plus, we have *Tall, Dark and Temporary* by Susan Connell, the latest in THE GIRLS MOST LIKELY TO... miniseries; *The Love Twin* by ultrasensuous writer Patty Salier; and Judith McWilliams's *The Boss, the Beauty and the Bargain.* All as irresistible as they sound!

I hope you enjoy January's selections, and here's to a very happy New Year (with promises of many more Silhouette Desire novels you won't want to miss)!

Regards,

Melissa Senate

Melissa Senate
Senior Editor

Please address questions and book requests to:
Silhouette Reader Service
U.S.: 3010 Walden Ave., P.O. Box 1325, Buffalo, NY 14269
Canadian: P.O. Box 609, Fort Erie, Ont. L2A 5X3

ANNE McALLISTER

THE COWBOY STEALS A LADY

SILHOUETTE *Desire*®

Published by Silhouette Books

America's Publisher of Contemporary Romance

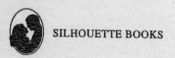

SILHOUETTE BOOKS

ISBN 0-373-76117-1

THE COWBOY STEALS A LADY

Books by Anne McAllister

Silhouette Desire

*Cowboys Don't Cry #907
*Cowboys Don't Quit #944
*Cowboys Don't Stay #969
*The Cowboy and the Kid #1009
*Cowboy Pride #1034
*The Cowboy Steals a Lady #1117

Silhouette Special Edition

*A Cowboy's Tears #1137

*Code of the West

ANNE McALLISTER

was born and raised in California, land of surfers, swimmers and beach volleyball players. She spent her teenage years researching them in hopes of finding the perfect hero. It turned out, however, that a few summer weeks spent at her grandparents' in Colorado and all those hours in junior high spent watching Robert Fuller playing Jess Harper on "Laramie" were formative. She was fixated on dark, handsome, intense, lone-wolf types. Twenty-nine years ago she found the perfect one prowling the stacks of the university library and married him. They now have four children, three dogs, a fat cat and live in the Midwest (as in "Is this heaven?" "No, it's Iowa.") in a reasonable facsimile of semiperfect wedded bliss to which she always returns—even though the last time she was in California she had lunch with Robert Fuller.

For Jason,
who answers all my questions
no matter what they are!
Everyone should have a friend like you.

One

Shane Nichols was at loose ends.

His older brother, Mace, could have told you that was a dangerous situation. But then, Mace had known his little brother for all of Shane's thirty-two years. Mace remembered the tipped-over outhouses, the burrs under the saddles, the superglue in Ms. Steadman's pencil box, the itching powder in old man Houlihan's underdrawers. And, of course, he remembered the chicken....

So when the doctor told Shane to cool it, Mace would have advised him to follow up his advice by doing something about it—like tying Shane to a bed.

Of course Doc Reeves didn't know Shane like Mace did. So all he said was that it wasn't every day a guy had his thumb sewn back on. These things took a while to heal. In the meantime, Shane should kick back and relax, take a little time off, enjoy life instead of busting his butt going down the road from rodeo to rodeo to rodeo.

Good advice as far as most guys were concerned.

Not the best for Shane.

He needed to be involved, on top of things. That was how he'd lost his thumb in the first place, of course—in a nasty encounter with a loose trailer, a spooked horse and some rigging. He'd been helping out—and he'd paid the price.

Fair enough. He would do anything for a friend. But he was tired of paying. He'd been kicking back and relaxing for three weeks now, wearing out his welcome at his brother's small ranch just outside Elmer, Montana. Going stir-crazy.

He had helped Mace go over the herd books, discussing ad nauseam the finer points of every one of Mace's steers and mamma cows. They could have spent another lifetime on it as far as Mace was concerned.

It drove Shane up the wall.

He enjoyed plate after plate of his sister-in-law Jenny's home cooking. She made him every one of his favorite foods. He could have grown fat and lazy just enjoying the comforts of home. After all, the ranch, though not large, was a damn sight bigger and more comfortable than the truck camper he was used to.

But bigger only meant he could spend his time pacing the rooms.

He had adoring nephews Mark and Tony to play with, to tell "goin' down the road" rodeo stories to. And he basked in their hero worship at the same time that he itched to get back on that very road. He had his six-year-old niece, Pilar, willing to entertain him with recitals of "Row, Row, Row Your Boat," on the piano whenever he said the word—which was fine for the first hundred and fifty times—but not forever.

This was beginning to feel like forever.

And Shane Nichols was not a forever kind of guy.

He was a mover, a shaker, a "do it now, regret it later" man.

He needed drama. High stakes.

He didn't want to row his boat anymore that week; he wanted a hundred-and-fifty-horsepower Evinrude. He didn't want to tell bull-riding stories; he wanted to ride one! He didn't want cozy fires and early bedtimes.

He wanted lights. Noise. Action.

That was why he ended up at The Barrel in Livingston that cold January night. It was the first time he'd been in a bar since the accident. There hadn't been a lot of point. He couldn't drink.

"Bad for the circulation," Doc Reeves told him, when he'd finally let Shane out of that Portland hospital three weeks before. "Gotta get as much blood to that thumb as we can. So...no alcohol. No coffee."

Next thing you knew he'd be saying, "No women," Shane had thought glumly.

It didn't take a medical degree to realize that blood pooling in another specific part of his body would detract from the red stuff that was supposed to be healing his thumb. Fortunately he got out of there before old Reeves had time to think of that!

Not that Shane was overloaded with women.

Not at the moment, anyhow.

He'd had his share of buckle bunnies, the rodeo groupies who made a point of chatting him up in a hundred bars across America. He'd had them bat their eyelashes at him and write their phone numbers on grocery receipts and cocktail napkins and—once—on the leather label on the hip of his jeans.

"But darlin', I won't be able to read it there," he'd protested.

The girl had giggled and shown him deep dimples, then brushed a kiss across his lips. "I know, sweetheart. But every time you take your pants off, you'll think of me."

He thought of her now. The blood in his thumb was considering making a move. For all the good it would do. Shane hadn't had a woman in so long it hurt.

And if watching his brother smooch with Jenny every day was difficult, knowing what they were doing when he wasn't watching was ten times worse!

He could tolerate all their lovey-dovey stuff for short amounts of time—Christmas, say, or a brief weekend stopover.

But three weeks!

No sir.

A guy could only allow all his blood to go to his thumb for just so long! Shane was already past it.

Way past.

He needed a distraction. And that had brought him to The Barrel, where he'd been delighted to find his old rodeo buddy Cash Callahan deep in a bottle of whiskey.

Shane looked longingly at the whiskey, then took another long swallow of ginger ale.

"*Ginger ale?*" Cash had looked disbelieving when Shane ordered it.

"Doc's orders," he'd said then.

Now, after his third glass, he was no nearer to being distracted, and his thumb was throbbing. He was beginning to think disobeying orders just a little might not hurt.

But every time he thought it, he remembered he wanted to ride again.

He didn't know what he would do if he couldn't ride again. His whole life had been rodeo since he'd been in high school. He'd graduated only because he knew his brother would've likely taken a belt to him if he hadn't. But the minute he had his diploma in hand, Shane had lit out to make his name in the rodeo world.

He might not be another Jim Shoulders or Tuff Hedeman, but he'd been to the National Finals Rodeo seven times. He'd finished second the year his old buddy Taggart Jones had won the Bull Riding World Championship. Twice he'd finished third.

Those didn't count, of course. The gold buckle was what counted. But he could still win the gold buckle, he told himself, *if he could ride.*

He had to ride. It was his life.

He kept working on the ginger ale.

Cash kept working on the whiskey.

"Don't see why she couldn'ta waited," he muttered, head bent over his glass.

Shane, who'd thought they'd been talking about the gelding Cash had drawn in Denver, said, "Huh? She who? Waited for what?"

"Milly." Cash jerked his head toward the group of women sitting at one of the tables by the window at the front.

Shane had seen them first thing when he'd come in. With women on his mind, he'd been quick to size them up. Check them out.

There were four of them, eating and talking and laughing. They didn't seem to be doing much drinking. He saw two beers and two soft drinks. He'd seen the same beers and the same soft drinks when he'd come in an hour before. Obviously no serious drinkers there.

"Who's Milly?"

"My girlfriend. *Ex*-girlfriend." Cash poured himself another whiskey from the bottle he'd got the bartender to leave next to his glass. He tipped the glass and downed the whiskey in a gulp, then smacked the glass back down on the counter again. "Damn her."

Shane eased around so he could study the women more easily. He wouldn't have thought any of them was Cash Callahan's type. From what Shane remembered, Cash preferred his women brash and blowsy.

None of these women fit the bill.

They all looked cheerful and wholesome and like they didn't belong in The Barrel at all.

"What're they doing here?"

"Celebrating," Cash muttered into his glass.

Shane lifted a quizzical brow.

"It's a tradition," Cash said. "Local girls do it. Come to The Barrel with their girlfriends just before they get married."

"How come?"

Cash shrugged. "How the hell should I know? Damn fool notion if you ask me. Milly says it started when some ol' gal dared another one to check out the rest of the men before she tied the knot. Tempting fate, she calls it."

Cash poured himself another shot, thumped the bottle down again and gulped the whiskey. "Not likely." He scowled in the direction of the table of women.

Shane nursed his ginger ale and studied them, too. "Interesting notion," he said. "Never heard of such a thing in Elmer. Of course, we only have the Dew Drop up there. Not that many fellas worth lookin' at."

"Only takes one." Cash's knuckles went white as his hand closed around the bottle once more. He didn't take his eyes off the women at the table.

None of them looked at him.

"Which one's Milly?" Shane asked.

"The pretty one." Cash didn't take his eyes off the glass in front of him. "Long dark hair. Green eyes."

Shane picked her out at once. Not that he was close enough to see her eyes, but there was only one pretty one. She'd caught his eye at once. And yes, she had lots of long dark hair for a guy to tangle his fingers in. But it was her smile, her laughter—a throaty musical laugh—that caught Shane's immediate attention.

He had no idea what she found amusing. But her lively smile, her genuine enjoyment of whatever one of the other women was saying, was contagious. It made Shane smile just to look at her.

"Yeah," he said, properly appreciative, "she's somethin', all right."

"She's that," Cash agreed grimly.

"How come she's your ex, then?"

"'Cause she got tired of waiting." Cash swirled the whiskey in his glass, then took a swallow and shut his eyes. Shane, watching him, could almost feel the burn in his own throat.

"Just like a woman," Cash muttered. "I'da waited for her. I'da waited till the cows came home for her. But no, she didn't want to wait. Said life was passin' her by, said all her friends were gettin' married, when were we gettin' married? Hell, do I look like I'm ready to get married?" He glared defiantly at Shane.

Obediently Shane shook his head. "Nope. Sure don't."

No more than he was ready himself. Marriage was something that happened to other people.

"Eventu'ly, I told her. We'll do it eventu'ly," Cash went on. "Gimme time, I said. Hell, I wasn't askin' for forever! Then last summer a friend of hers was gettin' married and they came here for their damned ol' girls' night out before the wedding, and she met *him*."

"Him?"

"Dutton. Mike Dutton. God's gift to women...or at least to Milly Malone. She's marryin' him Saturday."

"Whoa."

"That's what I said. Didn't do me a damn bit of good." Cash finished the whiskey and glowered in the direction of the women at the table. "She tol' me to take a hike. Tol' me I'd lost out. Lost her." His fists clenched and he started to stand, wavered and plopped back on the bar stool again. "Hell," he muttered. "'S hell."

"I reckon," Shane said sympathetically, though he frankly thought Cash ought to be celebrating having escaped the preacher's noose.

"It is," Cash affirmed. "Don't make a bit a sense. She doesn't love him! She loves *me!*"

"Course she does," Shane agreed soothingly. He was always ready to support a buddy. And, hell, it was probably true.

Cash Callahan was a good-looking son of a gun. Dang near every woman he smiled at fell head over fanny for him. Shane didn't know Mike Dutton from a hole in his shorts, but he'd be willing to bet Dutton didn't hold a candle to a guy like Cash.

"She'll be sorry." Cash rested his elbows on the bar and propped his head up with his fists. "She'll be damn sorry. She'll wake up Sund'y mornin' married to the jerk an' realize she made a mistake. But then it'll be too late.

'S all ready too late," he said, his words slurring. He put his head down on the bar.

"It's never too late," Shane said flatly. "She's not married yet. Talk to her. Tell her—"

"She won't listen." Cash's eyes closed. He wiggled his brows and managed to get them open again. "Tried."

"Make her listen. Insist." It was the only way to handle a woman. Firmly. Shane knew that.

"Yeah, right." Cash sighed. "I'd stop the weddin' if I was gonna be here," he said wistfully. "She'd have to listen then."

Shane grinned. "Reckon so." He shot a quick glance in the direction of the laughing woman.

She looked his way, too, then let her gaze skate quickly over him to land on Cash. She gave him a longer, almost pitying look, then deliberately turned back to her friends with a smile.

Shane heard her laugh. Was she enjoying Cash's misery? He felt his annoyance rising. He would like to see her face when Cash stood up in a pew and called out his objection!

"Why don't you?" he said eagerly.

"Can't. Drew me a great bronc down in Houston. Deliverance." He said the horse's name reverently.

Shane whistled. "That is a good 'un." There were a handful of sure money broncs in the rough stock trade. One of them was Deliverance. If he could stay on, a guy could win big on a horse like that.

Cash nodded solemnly. "So I can't stay." He shrugged. "If she'd wait, I could be back on Tuesday...."

She wouldn't wait.

Cash knew that. Shane knew that.

She'd go right ahead and marry ol' Dutton just because Cash wouldn't be there to stop her. It was a damn shame the way females were so all-fired impatient all the time.

Shane glared at the women on his friend's behalf.

The one with the long dark hair—Milly—met his gaze for another instant, then once more looked quickly away.

Guilt, Shane thought. Served her right.

There wasn't a finer guy in the world than Cash Callahan. He might be a little footloose sometimes. He might drink a little too much whiskey on occasion. He might think a good bronc was worth driving to Houston for. But he'd be there when the chips were down—if she really, really needed him. Shane knew that.

Didn't Milly?

Shane shook his head, disgusted.

"'Bout ready to hit the road?" Dennis Cooper, one of Cash's traveling partners, sidled up to the bar.

Wordless, Cash stared at the almost-empty bottle. Then, slowly, he eased his body around so he could get a look at the women at the table once more. They were laughing and talking. Not one—especially not the pretty one, Shane noted—paid any attention to him.

Cash sighed.

Dennis glanced at his watch. "We better be makin' tracks if we're gonna get out ahead of the storm."

"What storm?"

"Mark's been listenin' to the radio. Says there's a big one comin'. Blowin' in by morning, they say. So I say it's about time we headed south."

Cash poured the last of the whiskey into his glass and swirled the liquid, staring into it. "Guess so," he said. "Ain't nothin' left for me here."

He shut his eyes, tipped his head back and drained

the glass. Shane watched his friend's Adam's apple bob,
watched his lips press together in a tight, pained line.

Then Cash opened his eyes, blinked rapidly and
shoved himself to his feet. "Let's go," he muttered. He
gave Shane a soft jab to the upper arm. "Take it easy."
A pained grin quirked one corner of his mouth. "Don't
do anything I wouldn't do."

Shane grinned at that. "Leavin' the field wide open,
aren'tcha?"

Cash laughed. "Damn straight."

Then he tugged his hat down tight on his head and
squared his shoulders. Bow-legged, swivel-hipped, Cash
followed Dennis toward the door.

Shane watched to see if Milly would look at him as
he passed.

Would she watch him walk out of her life? Would she
feel his pain? Share it?

As he approached their table, Cash turned his head to
look at the women. It was no furtive glance, no quick
look. He kept his eyes glued on them as he passed.

They continued to laugh and talk, not even pausing.
The dark-haired one even lifted her glass in a toast.
Shane heard throaty, cheerful, musical laughter. He
knew damn well whose it was.

Cash reached the door, stood there.

Then the laugh came again.

Shoulders hunched, his head bent, Cash went out. The
door banged shut behind him.

As soon as he had, the long-haired beauty looked up.
Her gaze went to the door. A sad look crossed her face.
She sighed, then turned back to the other women and
said something. Then unhappily she shook her head and
took a long swallow of beer.

So she did have feelings.

Shane took a long swallow of flat ginger ale.

It was something to think about.

He thought about it. All night.

He made up his mind. He was going to save her from making a huge mistake.

It was the only thing to do.

She obviously had no intention of saving herself. She hadn't called the wedding off.

Shane hung around town the next day and listened to the gossip. Waited. Watched. Hoped. But nothing happened. The wedding was on.

It started to snow. Shane turned up the heater in his truck. Milly came out of the florist's shop around noon. She put flowers in the van emblazoned with the words Poppy's Garden and drove away.

"Where's Milly goin' in the florist's van?" he asked the girl who worked in the hardware store across the street.

"She works there," the girl said, not looking up from the cartons she was stacking.

After she made deliveries for the florist, Milly went to an apartment over a book shop. He followed. Shane supposed that was where she lived. He wondered if he ought to just go up and knock on her door and introduce himself, then try to make her see what a mistake she was making.

Yeah, sure. Like he could talk her out of it if Cash couldn't! Besides he'd never been very good at verbal stuff. Action was more his style.

So what was he going to *do*?

He was still pondering that when she left the apartment and headed back to the florist's. He went after her. She left there at closing time with another one of the girls he remembered seeing at The Barrel. They got into the florist's van and drove away down the snowy street.

Shane followed them to a church. A whole lot of other people were already there. They all went in. Shane sat outside in his truck and watched and waited. He knew what they were doing—rehearsing.

Time was getting short. And the snow that had begun in the morning was piling up and coming down even harder now. An hour later, when they all came out again, there was already seven or eight inches of it on the ground.

As Shane watched, Milly and the rest piled into their vehicles and headed off in the same direction.

Shane followed. They went into a steak house called Huggins's, on the edge of town. There Shane gave up sitting in his truck and went in to sit at the bar. From there he could see the private dining room they'd all entered. He nursed a whole series of ginger ales and tried to figure out what to do.

He was on his fourth when all of a sudden Milly came out of the dining room, heading for the rest room. Her eyes met his.

For an instant everything stopped. The laughing. The talking. The clink of glasses. The click of ice cubes.

And his heart.

His *heart?*

Shane coughed. He gave himself a quick shake and sucked in a deep breath. No, not his heart. His heart was just fine, thank you very much. Beating like it always did. Maybe a little faster even. Certainly it hadn't stopped.

There was too much smoke in the room. Too little air. He'd been thinking too hard. He looked away.

She hurried past.

He gulped the rest of his ginger ale and signaled for another. He downed it determinedly moments later when she went back. She didn't look at him. He didn't look at her. He knew what she looked like, for God's sake!

He needed a plan, that was all.

He ought to leave, forget the whole thing. It was insane, sitting here, hovering. But he couldn't just let her marry the wrong man, could he?

Just then the party broke up and, laughing and talking, Milly and her friends went out.

Shane thumped his glass down, tossed some bills on the bar and followed.

Cash would stop her if he was here, Shane assured himself.

But Cash was in Houston now, getting ready to make the ride of his life. He couldn't do what needed to be done.

So Shane would do it for him.

In the end it was easier than he thought.

A guy who made his living based on how successfully he dealt with eight-second episodes of bovine mayhem learned pretty quick that if he was going to win and keep on winning he had to take advantage of every split-second opportunity that presented itself.

When Milly and the girl from the florist's shop split off from the rest of the rehearsal dinner guests and climbed into the van, Shane got in his own truck, waited until they turned the corner, then took off after them.

The storm Dennis had wanted to miss had arrived at full force. Now, tucking his casted hand between his arm and his chest, Shane gripped the steering wheel with his good hand and plowed through the snow as he followed the van. Where the hell were they going at this time of night?

The answer was obvious almost at once. Back to the florist's shop.

Shane pulled in at the far end of the block, cutting his headlights, but letting the engine idle as he watched them get out and go up to the door of the shop.

Seconds later they went in and the shop lights went on. They weren't going to put together flowers now, were they?

But just then the door opened again and they came out, this time bearing some of floral arrangements that they struggled to carry through the snow to the van. Milly almost fell with hers.

Shane shook his head. What the hell was she doing? Arranging the flowers for her own wedding?

He waited. It took them four trips to finish. Then they shut the lights out in the shop and got back in the van. When they turned the corner, he pulled back out onto the snow-covered street and began to follow once more.

There was almost no one on the road. Everyone with good sense had got off the streets long ago.

Shane crept along, staying back far enough so that only their brake lights were visible in the snow. They didn't go far. And by the time he came to the corner where they'd turned, he knew where they were going, and yes, apparently she was doing the flowers for her own wedding.

They pulled up beside the church and got out to unload. When they finally disappeared inside, Shane drove his truck closer and parked.

He had just cut the engine when they came out again. With their hands empty, they laughed and swirled around, their arms outstretched.

Through the fogged-up windshield Shane could just catch a glimpse of snowflakes catching in Milly's hair as she spun.

He couldn't hear her laugh, but he could imagine it. The memory of that throaty musical tone sent a shaft of longing right through him.

"Damn." He shrugged his bottom along the cold seat of the truck, trying to find more room in his suddenly snug jeans.

He really had to find himself a woman! It wasn't like him to lust after another guy's girl. There were plenty of women to go around, for heaven's sake.

Still he couldn't seem to stop himself from reaching forward with his gloved hand and rubbing the moisture off the inside of the windshield so he could see better.

The women made another trip and then another. Once they glanced down the street toward where he was parked, and Shane eased himself down low in the seat, hoping they wouldn't notice him, then breathed a sigh of relief and straightened up when they turned and went back in.

They had just come out again when Shane saw a pair of headlights in his rearview mirror. A light-colored Chevy crept past him through the snow and pulled up behind the van.

The door opened, and a lanky young man got out. Shane recognized him from the rehearsal dinner. He was blond and hatless, and he was grinning.

The groom?

Shane's teeth came together with a snap.

Then as he watched, the fellow picked up the other girl and swung her around and around. Shane breathed easier. Not the groom. The best man, then. So fine. He didn't care about that.

As he watched, the guy set the other girl down, and the three of them carried the last of the flowers into the church. The heavy door swung shut behind them.

Shane didn't move. He waited.

And waited.

For what? he asked himself for the thousandth time. Was he going to sit there all night?

No, of course not. He was going to make her see sense, make her see that Mike Dutton, whoever he was, was the wrong guy for her.

How did *he* know this Dutton guy was the wrong man?

Shane's fist clenched on the steering wheel. He just *knew*, that's all!

The door to the church opened and the guy and the girl who wasn't Milly came out. She turned back, said something over her shoulder, then nodded, waved and shut the door.

The blond guy looped his arm over her shoulders and they headed toward the van. As Shane watched, they got in and drove away.

Milly remained in the church alone.

Shane got out of his truck.

Suddenly the door to the church opened and Milly came out.

Once more that night their gazes met.

He saw a look of recognition on her face—at first startled, then wary, then cautiously smiling.

He liked her smile. It made him smile back. It made his heart kick over in his chest.

"You're the guy who was with Cash," she said tentatively.

Right. Cash. *Remember Cash,* he told himself.

"Er, yeah. I gotta talk to you about that," he said. His voice sounded a little ragged.

"Cash is an idiot," she said flatly, smile fading, eyes flashing.

She was close enough now that Shane could see the

color of her eyes. They weren't really green like Cash had said. They were more hazel, but lit with green fire.

A man could get burned on a woman with eyes like that—and love every minute of it.

"He just sat there—like a bump," she said. "I can't believe he didn't say something! Do something!"

"Cash?" Shane stared at her. "What about you? Why didn't *you* do something?"

"Me? Why should I? It's his problem." She started to brush past, then turned and looked back at him. "Or did he think sending you around to spy on us was enough?"

Shane felt a sudden heat in his cheeks. "Spy on you? I never —"

"I saw you," she informed him. "I saw you at The Barrel. I saw you at Huggins's. I saw you park down the street from the shop. I saw you following us here. You were spying."

Shane scowled at her, his face burning. But he couldn't deny it.

"So, what're you going to do now? Report back to him?" Her tone was scornful.

Shane gritted his teeth. His thumb throbbed.

She sniffed and looked down her nose at him. "Oh, I forgot," she said disdainfully. "You want to talk. Go ahead. Talk."

Shane Nichols knew a dare when he heard one. And he'd never heard one he could refuse.

"Too late for talkin'," he said. "Way too late."

And he reached out, picked her up, slung her over his shoulder and headed for his truck.

Two

"**W**hat the—!"

But Shane wasn't listening.

He ignored her protests, ignored her fists thumping on his back, ignored the furious kicks of her legs, except one which came far too close to a certain vulnerable part of his anatomy, and kept right on walking.

Anchoring her butt with his casted hand, he wrenched open the door to his camper with the other, then hauled her forward and let her slide down the front of him. He sucked in his breath at the feel of her, dodged a fist swung at his head and pushed her in through the camper door, slamming it hard.

"Let me out of here! Hey! You! Let me out!" She pounded so hard the door shook.

Cursing the cast on his thumb, Shane fumbled with the latch to lock it.

"Damn you! Open this door!" The whole truck started to shake now.

In spite of himself, Shane grinned. "Not on your life!"

There was a moment's stunned silence, as if she hadn't expected him to answer. Then the camper stopped shaking, and she said in a calmer voice, "Let me out."

"No."

"Why not? What are you doing? You can't do this!" Her calm was fast deserting her.

"I just did."

"You can't! I've got work to do! I haven't finished."

"You're finished."

"The flowers—!"

"Flowers don't matter, do they, if there isn't gonna be a wedding?"

There was total stunned silence.

Shane smiled, letting her digest that fact. He waited, still smiling. The silence went on. And on.

Then, "What do you mean there isn't going to be any wedding?"

"Stands to reason, doesn't it?" he said cheerfully. "Can't be a wedding without a bride."

Now the silence was deafening. Well, at least he'd shut her up, Shane thought, satisfied.

"No...wedding?" She sounded faint.

He felt a moment's qualm at the sudden weakness in her voice, but squelched it promptly as he remembered Cash's misery and her own despairing look when he'd walked out with Dennis that night.

This was what she wanted, damn it! She just couldn't seem to make herself do it. Neither she nor Cash had been able to help themselves.

Shane was the only one who seemed capable of handling things around here.

"No wedding," Shane said firmly. "It's for your own good," he reminded her.

"My own good?"

He was pretty sure he heard disbelief—and something else...nervousness? panic?—in her voice. He steeled himself against it.

After all, what did she know? She'd been dumb enough to get herself engaged to the wrong man in the first place!

"Your own good," he affirmed. "Now you just sit tight there, darlin'. Don't worry 'bout a thing, and I'll get this show on the road."

He started to walk toward the front of the truck.

"Wait!" she yelped.

Shane stopped. "What?"

Her voice came to him, muffled through the fiberglass of the topper. "You're serious? You're taking me away just until the wedding's over?"

The nervousness was still there in her voice, but she sounded almost hopeful now. Shane reckoned she'd come to her senses at last.

About time. Except... "There isn't gonna be a wedding. Remember?"

"Oh. Right." Her voice wobbled a little. "I forgot."

Shane rolled his eyes. Obviously she wasn't the brightest bulb in the chandelier. Clearly it was that hair and those eyes that Cash found so appealing, not her intellect.

Well, in some women—like this one—that would be enough.

Was enough.

Something he shouldn't be thinking about, he reminded himself firmly. He sucked in a deep breath. "You just settle down there on one of those bunks an' relax."

"Relax? While I'm being kidnapped?"

"You're not bein' kidnapped. You're bein'—" he groped for the right word "—commandeered."

"Commandeered?" There was a wealth of doubt in that one word.

"Whatever." He hunched his shoulders against the sting of the snow. "I'm not gonna stand out here in a damn snowstorm and argue with you. This ain't the ransom of Red Chief, you know. Just sit tight now and let me get movin'."

Moving where?

Kidnapping, no *commandeering,* women wasn't something he did every day. Since he hadn't intended to, until she'd virtually dared him, he didn't have a clue about where to take her.

He could hardly take her back to Mace and Jenny's.

His brother was pretty tolerant. But even after he explained why he had Cash's girlfriend locked in the back of his camper, Shane doubted Mace would give his wholehearted approval. And Jenny would undoubtedly figure he was setting a bad example for the children.

So what did that leave?

He couldn't take her to a motel. The minute he turned his back, she would pick up the phone and call for help.

But he couldn't keep driving around, either. Not in weather like this.

He didn't know how much longer he would be able to keep going. The snow was coming so hard and thick and fast that by the time he reached the outskirts of

Livingston and was headed north into the valley he could barely see.

He had to find somewhere to stash her until the wedding was over, and he had to get there. Fast.

His eyes scanned what was visible of the foothills of the Bridgers, and that's when he remembered the cabin.

It was Taggart Jones's cabin. But Taggart was a kindred spirit. He wouldn't mind Shane using it for a while.

A lot of people had used that old cabin over the years. Mace and Jenny had lived there when they were first married. Mace had gone back there when he was sulking last year, trying to convince himself that Jenny was better off without him. Taggart had used the cabin himself when he was married the first time. And Jed McCall, another pal of Mace's, had lived there with his nephew before he'd married ol' man Jamison's daughter and moved to the neighboring ranch. Mace had said that Noah's brother's father-in-law had lived there for a while, too. Thus it was, Shane reasoned, available for anybody who needed it.

Even for a kidna—er, commandeering.

He didn't think anyone was using it presently. And once they were in, nobody would bother them. Nobody *could!*

There would be no phone. No paved roads. No way to walk out once they got in and he'd disabled the truck. And nobody likely to bother coming clear up there to look for a missing bride.

Shane drew a deep breath and let it out slowly, relieved to find such a perfect solution. Cash wasn't going to believe it when he came back and found Milly waiting for him.

See? There were some things even a guy with a bad thumb could do!

* * *

They weren't going to make it.

By the time he found the right road, there was so much snow that he hated to stop and open the gate for fear he would never get moving again. But the new tires he'd bought this fall gave him his money's worth, and the four-wheel drive he almost never used going down the road had paid off, so far.

But even so, it took more than an hour to get up a road that would have taken him fifteen minutes in good weather. Once he almost slid into the ditch. Twice he had to back up and take a run at a hill again.

He made one. He didn't make the next. They were almost there when his luck ran out.

He had to stop partway down a slope and walk over a rise just to be sure he was following the road at all. As he got out, the wind whipping down the mountains, blew enough snow to blind him. Hunching his shoulders, Shane tucked his bad hand between his ribs and his other arm and headed toward the ridge. Behind him he heard knocking on the camper's window.

Ducking his head and pulling down his hat tight, he ignored it and forged into the wind until he reached the top of the ridge. He began to think maybe he should have picked somewhere a little more accessible. He considered turning around.

A look back squelched that idea. He could barely see the truck. The wind had already obliterated the tracks it had made. The road was no more visible behind him than ahead of him.

He turned and studied what he could see of the landscape. It was, for the most part, white on white. There were few trees. He tried to gauge where the road would be in relation to them. When he thought he had figured it out, Shane turned and headed back.

Milly's face was pressed against the window. She knocked again.

He shook his head. This was no time for discussion.

She mouthed something, but her voice was garbled by the wind.

Shane shook his head again. He wasn't stopping to talk. Another half hour and this road was going to be impassable. Hell, it was probably already impassable.

He got back in the truck, started it, put it in gear, said a prayer, eased his foot down on the gas, edged forward slightly to get some momentum.

He got some. Enough to slide sideways into the ditch.

"Damn!"

Shane knew without even getting out to look that he didn't have a snowball's chance in hell of getting it back on the road by himself. Even if he dug for hours, he couldn't do it. And he couldn't dig for hours. Not with his thumb.

He said a rude word under his breath.

A tapping on the window behind his head made him jump. He sighed. They had all the time in the world for discussion now.

He got out and went around to the back. "What?"

"I need a bathroom."

He gave her a grim smile and extended a hand into the whiteness. "Be my guest."

Her cheeks flushed. "You're saying we're stuck."

Shane scowled. "It's only temporary."

"Like my abduction?"

He hunched his shoulders against a particularly sharp gust of wind. Not, he assured himself, against the accusing look in those bright hazel eyes of hers.

"Right," he said gruffly. He wasn't going to feel guilty, damn it. She ought to be thanking him. He was saving her from herself, wasn't he? It wasn't his fault it was snowing so damn hard.

"Come on," he said. "We can hike it. There's a bathroom in the cabin."

She jumped down, stood knee-deep in the snow next to him and looked around. "What cabin?"

"Over there. Just up the road." he said vaguely.

She looked into the swirling snowfall. "What road?"

Shane gritted his teeth. "Come on. I'll show you." He tucked his good hand around her arm and led the way.

"Is there a heater in this cabin?"

"You bet."

It wasn't on, of course. Neither, Shane realized when they finally stumbled in, was the water. So the plumbing wasn't working.

He could take care of both. But in the meantime...

"There's an old outhouse round back."

"An outhouse?" Her eyes widened.

He shrugged irritably. "I'll get the system going. In the meantime, you'll have to use what we have. Sorry it's not four-star accommodations. I didn't come up here and get things ready beforehand. It's not like I planned this, you know!"

Her wide eyes took on a look that was a disconcerting combination of guilelessness and mockery. "I'd never have guessed."

He couldn't light a match left-handed. He tried, God knew.

He flipped and fumbled and scraped and scratched. He had a hard enough time tearing them off the stupid packet. Then he couldn't get the right angle to strike them. They bent, they crumpled. Once, finally, one flickered, then promptly died as the wind gusted through the door when Milly came back from the outhouse.

"Damn it!" He had matches all over the floor.

She stared—first at him, crouched on the floor by the fireplace, then at the matches, then at his white casted, padded hand. "What happened?"

He knew she wasn't asking about the matches. "It's a long story."

She looked pointedly out a window at the blizzard raging beyond the glass as she shook off a blanket of snow. "I think we're going to have a while. So, I repeat, what happened?"

"I tore off my thumb."

She gaped at him. "On purpose?"

"Of course not! I was helping this girl unload, and a trailer hitch broke, and the horse spooked, and my thumb got caught and—" He shrugged. It wasn't the sort of injury that got a guy a lot of sympathy.

The light dawned. "You rodeo with Cash." Then, looking at his cast again, she said, "That's grisly."

"Uh-huh. But I picked it up. They sewed it back on." He turned back and fumbled with another match.

"You *picked it up?* Your thumb?"

What the hell else was he supposed to do? "Why not?"

She shuddered slightly, then held out her hand. "Give me those." She hunkered down next to him, took the matchbook out of his hand and deftly tore off a match. "Is this what we're lighting?" She nodded toward the wood and crumpled paper he'd laid in the grate.

"I thought it would warm the place up quick." He

grimaced at that bit of folly. "Then I was going to go out and work on the fuel tank."

She struck the match against the packet and cupped it in her palms, carrying it to the grate and touching it to the paper. It flickered and caught, spreading to the wood shavings that, thankfully, someone else had provided before they left. It moved to the kindling, settling, steadying.

The tiny pocket of warmth began to spread, too. Milly sat back on her heels and held her hands out to the fire, then breathed deeply, turned to Shane and smiled. "We did it."

"Yeah."

But he was getting warm, anyway, and it didn't have anything to do with the fire. Inside Shane, far from diffusing, the heat began to concentrate. All because of her smile.

He could see why Cash was head over heels for her. She had a way of looking at you that made you want to bust out grinning. It made a guy's chest expand. It made the tiny hairs on the back of his neck stand up. And other things, too.

Cash, he reminded himself. She belonged to *Cash*. He stood up abruptly. "Thanks."

"My pleasure," she said, apparently oblivious to his purely masculine reaction. She tossed her hair back and kept right on smiling as she looked up at him.

He wished she wouldn't. Toss her hair. Smile. Look at him. All of the above.

He backed away quickly, stumbling over his own boots in his haste to get out the door. "I'll just go see about that tank."

"If it takes a match, call me," she called.

Not on your life, sweetheart.

* * *

He didn't need a match outside.

Not to light the tank. Not to stay warm. Thanks to his body's persistent reaction to Milly, he was warm enough!

He got the fuel tank's supply valve turned on with no trouble. But he stayed out, anyway, giving himself a pep talk, reminding himself that he didn't poach on other guys' girls.

No way. No time. No how.

Only when he had the situation under control, when he figured he could walk back in and treat her with the indifference required, when he was confident he could ignore her, did he go back in.

He crouched down to look at the heater and discovered he needed another match to light the pilot. "Damn it!"

"Here." He jumped at the sound of her voice, and turned to see her stooping down behind him, a match already lit. "I'll do it."

She was close enough that he could feel her breath on his cheek. His body forgot his pep talk about indifference. Shane steeled himself against its demands and stabbed the button down.

Milly lit the pilot light, but didn't move away. She stayed right where she was. Her hair brushed his shoulder. Her knee touched his. He wondered if she could hear the hammering of his heart.

When he was sure there was enough voltage generated to hold the electromagnet down, Shane eased the button up. The pilot light stayed lit.

Her face lit up and she grinned. "Success!"

Distress, to Shane's way of thinking. He leaped up and practically dashed across to set the thermostat, shoving it up as high as it would go—not that he personally needed any heat at all!

"Shall we do the water heater while we're at it?" She looked at him expectantly.

"Sure," he managed. "Why not?"

He wanted to say, "Stop breathing down my neck!" He wanted to say, "Go away. I can do it myself." But he couldn't, and he knew it.

So they repeated their duet.

When that pilot light caught, too, she gave him another one of her smiles. Shane was prepared this time, steeling himself.

It helped. But not much.

He thought it would be better when she crossed the room and shed her parka. But it wasn't. Shane stared as she went to stand by the fireplace, arching her back and tipping her head back exposing her neck. Her eyes shut. Her hair tangled in loose waves down her back, drops of snow melting and making the fire spatter when they fell into it. Her breasts peaked against the soft dark green wool of her sweater, simply begging to be touched, to be caressed, to be nibbled and nuzzled.

By Cash.

"I gotta go," Shane blurted.

Her eyes snapped open. "Go?"

"Not for good," he said quickly. "Back to the truck. To…get my gear." *Get my bearings.*

"Do you want me to come, too?"

"*No!* I mean, no. You stay here. Keep warm." He just now noticed she was wearing only a pair of flats, not boots. "Why didn't you say?" he demanded, nodding at them. "I'd have carried you. You…weren't exactly dressed for, um…"

"Commandeering?" she suggested with a smile and an arched brow.

He felt like a fool. "It's for your own good," he muttered.

"Yes," she said, "it is."

He blinked. "You think so?"

"Absolutely."

He permitted himself a faint grin and a sigh of relief. "Well, I'm glad you came to your senses about that. An' I'll take you back like I promised. Just as soon as the wedding would be over."

"You think we'll be able to get out of here by then?"

Their gazes met. It was almost magnetic, this force he felt arcing between them. He had to start backing away in order not to cross the room just to be near her.

"I'll do my damnedest," he said. And he'd never meant anything the way he meant that.

Get a grip, he told himself. *You've seen a pretty girl before. You don't have to drool over this one.*

He wouldn't.

He would get his sleeping bag and stay the hell out of her way. Still, as he trudged back to where he'd left the truck, he wondered at a woman capable of inspiring such an intense reaction from so many men.

Cash, who could take his pick of a thousand buckle bunnies, only wanted this one. Mike Dutton, too, obviously wanted her badly enough to marry her.

And Shane—well, he hadn't had that intense a reaction to a girl since he was a sophomore in high school!

He wasn't a sophomore any longer, he reminded himself sharply. And thank God for that.

He was thirty-two years old. He'd seen New York and San Francisco and a thousand places in between. In thirteen years, he'd put more miles on his body than he wanted to count. He was all grown up, mature. He hadn't done anything downright foolish in years—well, months at least.

And he wasn't going to do anything dumb now.

It might have been maybe a little...er, impetuous... commandeering Cash's girlfriend this way, but he'd done it with the best of motives.

He was going to live up to those sterling motives now, he vowed as he dragged his sleeping bag out of the back of his truck and tucked his duffel bag under his arm.

He was going to go back to the cabin and be polite and proper and distant—every inch the gentleman his mother had often despaired he'd ever be.

But, he thought as he opened the door and felt an instant reaction to the sight of her sitting by the fire, her long dark hair billowing out, her face flushed, her eyes and mouth smiling, it sure as hell wasn't going to be easy.

Resolutely he stripped off his glove, then kicked the snow off his boots and stuck out his hand. ''I reckon we haven't been formally introduced. And since Cash isn't here to do the honors—'' he managed a rueful grin ''—I'll have to do 'em for him. I'm Shane Nichols.''

She rose and came across the room, smiling as she took his hand. ''Poppy Hamilton.''

''Pleased to—'' He stopped, mid-shake, and frowned. ''*Poppy?* But...Cash said your name was Milly.''

''Not...exactly.'' She looked apologetic. ''I've been trying to figure out a polite way to tell you...''

''Tell me what?''

She shrugged helplessly. ''You kidnapped the wrong girl.''

Three

The cumulative effects of concussion could do that to you.

Over the years you lost brain function, the ability to put two and two together, to comprehend the meanings of simple words. Shane had heard that. But he hadn't believed it until now.

"What did you say?"

It had to be all those concussions. It couldn't have been—

"What do you mean, *the wrong girl?*"

"I'm not Milly."

"Of course you're Milly!"

What the hell kind of game was she playing? Did she think he was going to take her back and trade her in on someone else if she denied her identity?

"But I'm not. For some reason you *thought* I was Milly." She looked at him hopefully. "You were trying to kidnap Milly,'' she clarified, when he just stared at her.

"I know who I was trying to kidnap!" he shouted at her. "And damn it, I told you, I wasn't *kidnapping* anyone!"

"Excuse me. Commandeering."

Shane nodded, justified.

But then she shook her head and gave him a pitying look. "So, consider me commandeered. But I can't change who I am. And I'm Poppy. Not Milly."

He glared at her, still stunned, and said the only thing he could think of. "Prove it."

She shrugged, then sighed. She crossed the room and got her parka and fished in the pocket, pulling out a wallet. She opened the wallet, crossed the room and handed it to him. "My license."

It was her, all right. Same sparkly eyes, same drop-dead gorgeous smile, same glorious hair. Who'd have thought a driver's license photo could look so damn good?

Then he looked at her name.

It didn't say Milly.

But it didn't say Poppy, either, he noted with considerable satisfaction. "This says Georgia," he pointed out. "Georgia Winthrop Hamilton."

She wrinkled her nose. "My real name. I'm named after my father."

He stared at her.

"As close as my mother would allow him," she explained. "I was their only child. The only one they were ever going to have, and they knew it. My father probably would have named me George if he'd thought he dared," she added a little wryly. "But my mother insisted on Georgia. And she called me Poppy."

"How do I know she didn't call you Milly?"

"Because there would be no reason to," she said, as if it were perfectly logical.

It wasn't to Shane. He didn't follow. There seemed to be a lot he wasn't following.

"My mother said that when I was a baby and I cried, my face got as red as Georgia O'Keefe's poppies. Ergo...my name." She gave a helpless shrug and a smile. "My mother had a certain sense of humor."

Apparently.

Shane thought a certain sense of humor would be a good thing right now. He tried to find his.

This girl wasn't *Milly?*

He tried thinking back over the evening with Cash at The Barrel. Cash was the one who'd been drinking; Shane hadn't. Now, if *he'd* been the one drinking he could see that maybe he'd made a mistake. But he hadn't touched a drop. He could still taste the ginger ale now, if he thought about it hard enough.

He shook his head. "But he said..." He was trying to remember what Cash *had* said.

The pretty dark-haired one. That was what Cash had said.

Well, there was only one pretty dark-haired one.

Or only one that Shane had seen.

He groaned. He shut his eyes and pinched the bridge of his nose. In his head he tried to reconstruct the scene. Two of the women had been blondes. The other two were brunettes. Both had long hair.

But only one of them was pretty.

The other girl was the one who'd driven away in the florist's van with the guy who'd showed up at the church.

The other girl was...

Milly?

"The one who drove off in the florist's van?" he said faintly, groping, praying, even at the same time he knew his prayers had already been answered—and that the answer wasn't yes.

The florist's van had been called something cutesy. Daisy's Flowers or Poppy's...

He groaned again, remembering bright red letters and what they'd said. Poppy's Garden.

"Milly," the girl in front of him agreed. "She borrowed my van."

He fixed her with an accusing stare. "You're the florist?"

"I'm the florist."

Shane was furious. "Then why'd she take the damn van?"

"Mike's buddies were going to decorate the car tonight. You know, the 'just married' crepe paper and tin cans stuff. They told him to leave it at the church. Milly came with me so we could do the flowers. She's been helping me in the shop. Then Mike came to pick her up, and I let them take my van for the night. I didn't need it. I only live a couple of blocks away—"

"In the apartment over the book shop," he said heavily.

"Exactly. I was going to walk home when I finished. But then you came along and—"

Shane's teeth came together with a snap. He yanked his hat off and threw it across the room.

He fixed Miss Georgia—*Poppy!*—Hamilton with a furious glare. "So why the hell didn't you say something, for God's sake? You *let* me do it!"

She looked indignant. "Like it's my fault now?"

He stalked a furious lap of the small room, then

stopped to glower at her some more. "Of course it is! You could have stopped me!"

"How? By protesting that I wasn't Milly? Would you have believed me?"

Shane's good fist clenched and unclenched. He didn't know whether he would have or not.

Probably...not.

He would have thought she was lying to prevent him from doing what they both knew needed to be done. And the very thought made him furious all over again!

He raked his fingers through his hair. He muttered under his breath. He said words that would have had his mother washing out his mouth with soap. He was pleased to see Miss Georgia—*Poppy!*—Hamilton's eyes widen. And then he was embarrassed at offending her.

He clamped his mouth shut. "Sorry," he muttered. He spun around and stared out the window into the blizzard. His mind whirled as fast as the snow outside.

As fast as his tires would spin if he were trying to get them out of the ditch. He wasn't going to be able to get them out of the ditch. They were stuck.

His shoulders slumped. His head drooped. His eyes shut. "Hell."

A tentative hand touched his back. He jumped.

"You meant well," she said gently.

He jerked away. "Uh-huh."

"It was...really sort of noble of you."

Shane snorted.

"Even though it wasn't your problem." She edged around so she was in his line of vision, but he still refused to look at her. "It was Cash's responsibility, you know," she said. "Not yours. Cash should have done something."

"He had to leave!"

"He always has to leave," Poppy said impatiently. "Milly was sick of it."

"So she marries someone else to make a point?"

"No, she marries someone else who doesn't have to leave. Somebody who shows her by his actions as well as his words that she matters more to him than some damn horse does."

"It was Deliverance," Shane argued.

"I don't care if it was Pegasus! No woman wants to come in second to one horse after another for her whole life."

"Not her whole life. Just until Tuesday."

Poppy rolled her eyes. "You just don't get it, do you? You're another one, just like Cash."

"I guess I am," Shane said stubbornly. "I've never met a woman yet, I'd stay around for if there was a bull worth ridin' down the road."

"Well, that's frank." Poppy blew out a long, slow breath. "So if Cash feels the same way, which he obviously does, why should Milly want to make a marriage with a man like that?"

"He loves her," Shane said stubbornly.

"He doesn't know what love is! And—" she sniffed "—obviously neither do you."

Shane looked at her, offended. "I'm not the one gettin' married!"

"Who'd have you?"

Oddly, that stung. He gritted his teeth. "You'd be surprised," he said through them.

In fact, though, he wasn't sure how many of the buckle bunnies he'd dated over the years had actually been smitten enough to want to hitch up with him long-term.

It didn't matter, 'cause he'd never asked!

"I would," Poppy agreed coolly. "Be surprised," she

added, in case he was too dumb to get the point. "But after tomorrow Cash can ride whatever horse he wants. Milly's going to marry Mike and be happy." She lifted her chin and defied him to dispute it.

He couldn't.

She was right.

Maybe not about the being happy part. Time would tell about that. But tomorrow, wherever Cash was, and whatever horse Cash was riding, or whether Cash liked it or not, Milly was going to marry Mike.

Because Shane had kidnapped the wrong girl.

He headed for the door.

"Where are you going?"

"To get the truck out. To take you back. We're not stayin' here."

"But it's stuck! It's snowing."

"No kidding," Shane said under his breath. But that was no excuse. He'd got them here in the snow. He could damned well get them out again.

"Wait!"

But he didn't wait. He stuffed his arms in his jacket as he went and fumbled with the zipper as he trudged through the snow. He heard Poppy—he could almost bring himself to think of her as *Poppy* now—bang out the door after him. He turned. "You don't have boots."

"I found an old pair by the chair."

From some previous occupant no doubt. Shane glanced back to see her clumping back after him in boots that were far too big for her. "Go on back and wait. I'll come and get you when I get it out."

But she didn't stop. She came right on. "No. If you're going to be an idiot again—"

"What do you mean again?" he growled.

But she didn't answer, just caught up with him and plunged on. It didn't matter. He knew what she meant.

"You have to promise, though," she panted as they walked, "not to try to kidnap Milly now."

"I think," Shane said through gritted teeth, "that I'm done with kidnapping at the moment."

She flashed a grin his way. "Good."

The truck was buried halfway up the doors in snowdrifts. He had to shove snow away from the back with his hand before he could open the door and get out the shovel. Poppy meanwhile cleared off the windshield and brushed off the hood. It was awkward shoveling with one good hand, and he didn't move very quickly or very efficiently. He was also aware that Poppy had finished brushing and stood watching him work.

"Want me to take a turn?" she asked him.

"No."

But eventually he had to stop, exhausted. And then she took the shovel and picked up where he left off. He felt useless, standing there, sweating and panting as he watched her struggle to move the heavy snow. In less than a minute he grabbed the shovel again. "I'll do it."

But the wind picked up and the snow swirled down. The more he shoveled, the less progress he made. Finally he said, "Come on. Get in. We can't keep digging in this. We might as well just give it a shot."

They clambered in and he gunned the engine. The wheels caught. The truck lurched. The wheels spun. The truck slid.

Shane cursed. He put the truck in first and rocked it forward, then in reverse and rocked it back, hoping to get some momentum, hoping to dig his way out.

He dug his way in instead. The tires whirred and whined in the snow, then dug into the dirt beneath. The truck settled deeper. He could smell the clutch as it began to burn. The truck stayed right where it was.

Finally he shut the engine off and banged his fist against the steering wheel. "Hell."

"It's all right," Poppy said.

It wasn't, but that didn't change anything. He felt a light touch and looked around to see her fingers on his sleeve.

"It is," Poppy repeated. "Come on. Let's go back to the cabin."

He put the shovel back in the camper. They climbed up the slope and over the hill and down the other side. There Poppy stumbled and he grabbed her, catching her before she could fall. "Careful!"

She turned her head and smiled at him, and he felt the same stab of attraction he'd been fighting since the first time he saw her.

And that's when he realized that she wasn't Cash's girl anymore.

It was like being hit over the head.

He looked at her again. Narrowly, assessingly. Hopefully. And she looked back—and yes, it was in her eyes, too.

Shane started to smile.

He didn't care what Cash said, Poppy was definitely the "good-looking" one.

In fact, good-looking didn't even begin to cover it. Her luxuriant hair was only one part of her attraction. She had flawless skin—even reddened from being out in the wind, she looked not ruddy, but vibrantly alive. He liked her high cheekbones, her straight nose and generous mouth. He liked the spattering of freckles across her nose. They made her seem accessible, touchable.

He wanted to touch her. For now he snugged her arm through his and led the way back to the cabin.

It was blessedly warm when they got there this time. The fire in the fireplace had burned down quite a ways, so he added another log, more for atmosphere than for added heat, then said, "How about some food?"

She shook her head. "I'm not really hungry. I had a big dinner."

"Mind if I do?"

Shane had seen them carrying in big platters of food into the private dining room from where he'd sat nursing his ginger ale at the bar. They'd eaten prime rib and Huggins's special twice-baked potatoes. He'd eaten peanuts and a handful of chips while trying desperately to figure out what to do to save the day for Milly and Cash.

Obviously he should have spent more time eating and less time plotting.

"Not at all," Poppy said. "I'll be glad to help."

Shane grabbed a can of chili out of the cabinet, fished a can opener out of a drawer and stopped. He looked at the can, at the can opener, at his casted hand and gave a rueful shrug. "Guess you'll have to," he said.

Poppy took the can opener and opened the can. Shane watched, admiring her hands. They were slender with long fingers. He imagined them touching his cheek. He imagined nibbling on them one by one.

"Don't just stand there," she said briskly. "Get a pan."

Shane blinked, then flushed. "Right." He got the pan and set it on the stove. Poppy scooped the chili into it for him, then chopped it up with a spoon.

"I'll do this," she said. "Why don't you set the table?"

While he set the table, he asked her about Poppy's Garden.

"How'd you get to be a florist," he said to her.

"I like growing things. I like playing with color. I like saying things without words." As she spoke, her eyes were alight with eagerness. "Arranging flowers lets me do all three. I love it. It's like you're given all this natural beauty and then asked to create more."

"You been doing it long?"

"I've had my shop for three years. I worked there while I was in college, then bought it from the owner when he retired." She dished him up a bowl of chili and handed it to him.

Shane's brows lifted. "Pretty ambitious."

"It's what I wanted to do." There was a sudden firmness in her voice that made him understand some of the determination that was beneath those soft smiles. "And I wasn't wrong about that," she added almost as an afterthought. It made him wonder if there had been something else she *had* been wrong about, but he didn't ask.

"Looks like you made a success of it," he said warmly as he sat down and began to eat.

"Yes, I have." A smile touched her mouth again and she sat down across from him. Their glances caught once more. This time longer than the last. Deliberately Shane didn't break it. It was Poppy who first looked away.

"Where'd you go to school?" he asked her.

"Montana State. And you?"

"Didn't." A corner of his mouth quirked into a grin. "Barely managed to stand high school long enough to finish," he said frankly. "It wasn't that I was so stupid," he added. "It was more that I just didn't want to be there. You know how they say, 'Get a life?' Well, I had a life, and school was in the way. I tried to make it interesting, but when I did…well, let's just say they tended to get all hot and bothered.''

A smile touched Poppy's lips. "I can imagine."

"I doubt that," he said darkly and dug into his chili again. "Sure you don't want some?" he asked her.

"On second thought, maybe I will." She got up and walked to the stove to dish up a bowl for herself.

Shane sat there and enjoyed simply watching her move. He liked to watch women move. They moved so differently from men. There was a sinuousness about them, a grace that no man could come close to. When they moved they didn't seem to walk so much as flow.

Poppy Hamilton was no exception. She was extremely easy on the eyes. Her long legs reminded him of a colt's. Curvier, though. He could see the curves outlined in the wool of her slacks. He imagined them without the wool, warm and bare and wrapped around his hips.

A shaft of desire surged through him so sharply that he jerked and practically tipped the chair over. He flailed, grabbing for the table, nearly knocking over the chili.

"Are you all right?"

Embarrassed, he thumped all four chairs legs down solidly. "Fine. I'm fine! Just tipped the chair too far."

She gave him a worried look, then shrugged.

Shane cleared his throat. "You grow up around here?"

"Yes."

"How come I never saw you before? I've generally got an eye for a pretty girl." He flashed her a grin and was gratified when she blushed.

"I doubt if you would have noticed me," she said as she carried the bowl back to the table. "You're a lot older."

That wasn't what he expected her to say. Shane's brows drew down. "I am not!"

"I'm only twenty-five," Poppy said demurely.

"I'm thirty-two."

"See?" she said impishly. "A lot older."

Shane bristled, then realized she was laughing at him. He stabbed his fork into the bowl of chili. "You're actin' pretty juvenile, all right," he grumbled.

She grinned unrepentantly. She'd better not do much more of that grinning, he thought, not if she didn't want him picking her up caveman fashion and hauling her off to the bedroom.

"I guess thirty-two isn't *real* old," she said after a moment.

"Thanks," Shane muttered.

"Did you grow up in Livingston, too?"

"I grew up near Elmer. My brother has a ranch up there. I get back fairly often. Sometimes I go down to Livingston. I was there the other night 'cause I was goin' stir-crazy on the ranch."

"Because of your thumb? It's kept you tied down?"

He nodded. "Almost a month now. I hate it. I want to be doin' something. I guess I reckoned saving Milly for Cash was one thing I could do," he said a little ruefully. "Shows what a fool I am."

"No," Poppy said. Her voice was gentle.

They looked at each other. The temperature in the room seemed to go up a good ten degrees. Shane eased the collar on his shirt away from his neck. He shifted in his chair. He reached out his good hand and touched hers.

Hers were the hands of a woman who worked for a living. Her nails were short and unpolished, but neat. Smaller than his hands. Delicate. Yet capable, too. He could see that. He could imagine them arranging flowers, making slight adjustments. He could imagine them curling inside his fingers, brushing down his cheek.

She got up. "I could use a cup of coffee. How about you? If there is some?"

"Sure." It gave him the opportunity to study her some more. He finished his chili, then eased his chair back and crossed his feet at the ankle. Poppy scavenged through the cupboards looking for coffee and mugs.

"So if you grew up in Livingston and you're twenty-five, you must know Billy Adcock? He's about your age." Billy was a top-notch bronc rider, the younger brother of a friend of Shane's.

"I knew him. But he went to a different school. I didn't go to high school here. I went back east to prep school."

Back east? To prep school? He frowned. Was she the daughter of some Hollywood celeb? There were a few who owned big spreads down in the Paradise Valley. He tried to think if there were any Hamiltons in the movies.

Cripes, yes, he thought. There was. And his name was even George!

He gaped at her. "Your dad's the actor?"

She shook her head and laughed. "Not quite."

"Good." He gave a sigh of relief. He didn't want to think of her being one of "them"—one of the interlopers who came in and drove up land prices and commuted by jet to their day jobs.

The only other Hamilton he remembered, he didn't want to talk about. The judge did not figure in his fondest memories. He had, in fact, been responsible for the most humiliating experience in Shane's life. Fortunately the old coot was far too ancient to have a daughter Poppy's age.

"So, do you know Todd Clifton? Ray Setsma? Setsma and I used to rodeo together."

Poppy grinned. "Before he grew up, you mean?"

"Before he got tied down," Shane corrected gruffly. Though whether he liked it or not, there was an element of truth in what she'd said. Over the last few years Ray seemed years older than he was, although he was, in fact, a year younger. It was just that he'd got married ages ago, and now he and Lisa had three kids, or maybe even four.

"How long have you ridden bulls?" she asked him.

"All my life. Well, it seems like all my life, anyway. Guess I rode my first one when I was about thirteen. Before that I'd ridden sheep, cows, steers. You name it, if it had four legs and a tail, I was always willing to give it a shot. But once I got on a bull, well...that was that." Just thinking about it could get his adrenaline flowing. It was the biggest challenge. The greatest risk.

And when you did it...when you succeeded...God, there was no other feeling like it in the whole wide world!

He looked right at Poppy, a grin lighting his face like the grin he always wore when he made the buzzer. And she grinned back, and the current was almost electric between them.

Outside, the wind roared and the snow fell. Inside, the log settled in the grate and the coffee boiled and boiled. In the morning Milly was going to marry Mike and Cash was going to ride Deliverance.

And Shane didn't care about any of it.

Only about this.

Only about her.

"Oh! The coffee!" Poppy jumped and hurried to grab

the pot off the burner and fill two mugs. "It's pretty strong." She made a face.

"It's fine," Shane said and got slowly to his feet. "I'll let mine cool a bit and go make up the bed for you."

He went to the cupboard and took out the sheets and blankets he would need, then headed into the bedroom and as best he could, one-handed, made up the bed.

There was only one. It was a double, but not a big double. Fine for one person. Cozy for two. A smile touched his mouth.

When he went back into the front room, Poppy was doing up the dishes. She had her back to him, and her head was bent. He could see the nape of her neck peeking out where her hair had parted and fallen forward over her shoulders.

He walked up behind her and settled his hands at her waist. She stiffened, but she didn't shrug away. He could almost feel the tension vibrating in her, though. Exactly the way he could feel it vibrating in himself.

Need. Hunger. Desire.

He edged closer, drawn by the heat of her body. They touched. His hands slid clear around her, holding her lightly in his embrace. He pressed the lightest of kisses against the back of her neck.

She shivered.

"Bed's made," he said, his voice just a little husky.

For an instant she didn't move. For an instant they were still pressed together, man and woman, and he knew she could feel what her body was doing to his.

And then she turned with the very same graceful sinuousness that he had admired not long before, raised his arm and slipped under it, all the while smiling as she said, "You don't want to have to deal with my father."

"Tough guy, is he?"

She nodded. "The toughest."

Shane sighed. "Not as tough as a Hamilton I once knew."

"Who was that?"

"A judge. A century ago he'd have been a hanging judge." He grimaced at the memory. "He was a tough ol' buzzard. Righteous. Stern. Beetle-browed. Face like an ol' boot."

"Sounds charming," she said dryly.

"Not. He shoulda been a Marine drill sergeant. Prob'ly was in another life. He was a purely wicked old man. Made my life miserable."

"What happened?"

"Kid stuff. No big deal, really. At least I didn't think so. Everybody else seemed to, and, well...he was the judge on the case."

"Details?" Poppy urged.

Shane shook his head. "Nope. Suffice to say, I had a little too much school spirit."

Poppy looked intrigued. "And?"

"Hard-Ass Hamilton squashed it for me." And that was nothing but the truth.

Poppy laughed. "Sounds like something he'd do. Though I've never heard him called that before."

Shane was surprised she'd heard him called anything at all. He would have bet a thousand bucks she was far too straitlaced to have ever come up in front of a judge.

"You know ol' Hard-Ass?"

She nodded, still smiling. "He's my father."

Four

Her father had that effect on people.

Not the least, Poppy reflected as she lay between the cold sheets, herself.

The Honorable George Winthrop Hamilton was indeed a force to be reckoned with. Poppy ought to know. She'd been reckoning with him her whole life.

Not that he wasn't a good father. He was. He was thoughtful, intelligent, earnest, hardworking, determined and he had all the finesse of a steamroller when he made up his mind about what he wanted.

Or what he thought was good for her.

Born late in her parents' marriage—the child they'd always longed for and finally against all odds had— Poppy had forever been the focus of all her father's hopes and dreams.

For the first twenty years of her life, she had also been blessed with a mother who threw up roadblocks to prevent the judge from flattening everything in sight to make those dreams come true.

But after her mother's death, Poppy had been on her own.

She hadn't always done the best job. Oh, some things she'd done well enough. Like instead of going to Yale, her father's alma mater, she'd insisted on going to MSU when her mother had become ill. And she'd stuck to her botany major in the face of his opposition.

"How on earth will you get into law school with a degree in plants?" he'd demanded.

Of course, he hadn't known then that she wasn't planning to go to law school. But when, after graduation, she'd bought the flower shop, he'd got the idea. And been furious.

And wrong.

At least she'd been right about that. There were other areas of her life where she hadn't been quite so smart.

She hadn't, for example, been right about Chad.

It was, she thought, because of her initial success with her flower shop that she'd got involved with Chad Boston in the first place. She'd been heady with her accomplishments, giddy with the belief that making adult decisions really wasn't so hard after all.

And so she'd overlooked her first impression of Chad Boston—that he was just a little too forward, a little too confident, a little too...*interested* in her.

She should have known, she told herself afterward.

Men weren't generally falling all over themselves to go out with her. They thought she was pleasant and good company and some of them even flirted—like Shane—until they found out who her father was.

And then they vanished.

There was something about being the daughter of

Montana's twentieth century answer to "the hanging judge" that sent men heading for the hills.

Except Chad.

When Chad had learned whose daughter she was, he'd seemed pleased.

"A judge's daughter?" he'd said, and his smile had widened.

It almost seemed to make him seek her out. In retrospect she realized that was the truth. But at first she'd thought it was her own scintillating personality that had drawn him to her. And she'd been aglow with the idea that she had a real boyfriend at last.

A successful boyfriend, too. A real estate wheeler dealer. A man on the move.

An out-of-stater, to be sure. But Poppy didn't scorn recent arrivals the way some Montanans did. Although it turned out she should have scorned Chad Boston.

Her father had warned her. Generally not one to criticize her friends, he did wonder aloud at some of Chad's land deals.

"That young man know what he's doing? He can't divide that property, you know," he said to Poppy once.

But Poppy was confident that Chad knew what he was doing. And she was right—just not right about what it was she thought he was up to.

In fact, she didn't really have time to give it much thought. She had her own business to run. And when she wasn't busy in the shop, Chad was distracting her—wining and dining her, more or less sweeping her off her feet. It was a heady experience for a woman who'd never had a steady boyfriend.

She thought he was everything she'd ever wanted. And when he asked her to marry him, she said yes.

Fortunately before they got to the altar, the law got to

Chad. Even then, when the trouble began, she thought it was just that he didn't understand the covenants and that when he did, things would be all right. She didn't completely understand them herself. She suggested he talk to her father and get things straightened out.

"Don't need to," he'd said, dropping a kiss on her nose. "It'll all blow over. When people find out I'm the judge's son-in-law, they'll come around. Having a judge in the family is great for credibility." He'd grinned at her.

"But if it's illegal..." Poppy had protested.

"Nobody has to know that."

He'd been so smug. So sure of himself. Of her. And her father.

Bad judgment on his part.

Poppy knew her father even if Chad didn't. In Judge Hamilton's eyes, illegal was illegal—no matter who did it. And a man had to accept responsibility for his actions.

When Chad was arrested, he expected the judge would go to bat for him. He was sadly disappointed. So was Poppy. But not in her father. She was disappointed in her own judgment—and in the man she'd hoped to marry.

Chad plea-bargained and left the state.

A month later he wrote and asked if she would mind returning the ring he'd given her.

She didn't mind in the least.

She minded being a fool, though. She minded having made such a disastrous choice. It had been two-and-a-half years, and she hadn't dared make another one. She'd shut herself off from men since then, afraid she might do it again.

"You won't," her father assured her. "He was the bad apple in the bunch."

But Poppy didn't trust herself anymore.

"Fine," her father said, "I'll find a man for you."

She'd thought he was kidding until he started turning up with eligible men. It was embarrassing beyond belief.

She was polite to them, of course. But she found something wrong with each of them. This one was too tall. That one was too short. This one was too moody. That one had a boring job. She expected that before long he would stop looking.

And then last summer he'd had a mild heart attack. Poppy thought that might make him quit. And when the too tall, too short, too this, too that men stopped appearing, Poppy breathed a sigh of relief.

But she was wrong. He'd just become more serious. He was seventy years old and suddenly aware that he might not live to see Poppy settled and giving him grandchildren. He wasn't wasting time on 'probables' anymore. He was going for her perfect man.

Last Monday he'd appeared in her shop, beaming and rubbing his hands together, sporting the look reserved for when he'd put a criminal away for life. "Got him," he said.

Poppy, used to glee in judicial matters, had barely looked up from concentrating on the daffodils she was arranging. "Got whom?"

"Your perfect husband."

Poppy almost decapitated a daffodil. "What?"

"You heard me. And this one really is. He's not like all the others. He's exactly right." He looked at her for congratulations.

Poppy managed a wan smile, all the while strangling the scissors in her hands. She wished it was her father, or even better, her perfect husband, for she was reasonably certain that her father's notion of perfect husband material was not her own.

"J.R. Phillips," her father had said. "He's a lawyer. Went to Harvard. But he's Montana born and bred. His daddy owns a big spread up near Great Falls. J.R. used to cowboy for him. He's educated and a man of the land, both. Dark hair. Green eyes. Six feet tall. Fine-lookin' fella. You'll love him."

As if, Poppy thought, those were all the qualifications it took.

As far as her father was concerned they were. "He's coming Friday. You can come out to the house and fix dinner for him."

How like her father to think she would jump at the chance to show off her housewifely skills. "Sorry I can't."

His brows snapped together. "Why not?"

"Milly's rehearsal is Friday."

Her father heaved a sigh, then said, "Fine. Don't cook him dinner. Come by and meet him after the rehearsal."

"I can't. We're doing the flowers together, Milly and I. She works for me now, did I tell you? Anyway, after the dinner we're taking the dried arrangements over to the church and setting things up."

"If she's working for you, delegate. Let Milly do it."

"It's *her* wedding, Daddy. She's got other things on her mind. Besides, she doesn't have the experience."

"You're not going to get out of this, Poppy," her father said sternly. "If you won't come to the mountain, the mountain will come to you. I'll bring him to the wedding. I have an invitation for Judge Hamilton and guest," he said, forestalling her objection. "We'll be there. You can't miss the wedding."

And she wouldn't have—if Shane Nichols hadn't appeared out of a snowstorm and kidnapped her.

Bless his dear misguided heart.

Shane didn't know what a huge favor he had done her.

Poor guy, she thought now, tucking the blanket under her chin. He hadn't had a world-class day. He'd been more than a little disconcerted by her revelation that she wasn't Milly. But he seemed even more discomfited by the discovery that he had kidnapped "Hard-Ass" Hamilton's daughter.

Poppy smothered a giggle now as she recalled the look of horror on his face. And the deep red flush that followed.

She'd been charmed. She'd never met a man who blushed before.

Chad certainly hadn't.

Of course Chad had no shame. And maybe blushing wasn't all that commendable among men in general. But when it came to kidnappers, Poppy decided it was a positive character trait.

He had a few other positive traits as well. Like the most beautiful dark blue eyes she'd ever seen. And a lean, hard, handsome face. Chad's features had been almost classically beautiful, but Shane's had character, which she found even more attractive. He had an easy, confident masculine grace, too, telling her that women probably fell over like bowling pins if he so much as winked.

She wasn't surprised.

She wouldn't be averse—*if* she were that kind of girl. Not that there was any chance of him going to bed with her now!

Once she'd said, "He's my father," about Judge

"Hard-Ass" Hamilton, Shane had practically shoved her into the bedroom and slammed the door.

It was an extreme version of a reaction she was used to. The exact opposite of Chad's response. She found that she trusted it. Liked it.

Liked him.

She could well imagine a guy like Shane, one who seemed to leap before he looked and would do anything—even kidnap a bride, for a friend—would run afoul of the authorities now and again. She wondered what sort of "school spirit" had brought him before her father. Some sort of petty vandalism, no doubt. Lots of students, caught up in the fervor of school spirit, spray painted their school's name in public places.

She wondered if her father had made him scrub it off. She knew he'd done that. Her father believed in the punishment suiting the crime.

What would her father do if he knew Shane had kidnapped her?

The very thought made her smile.

Was that what Shane was worried about?

She would have to assure him that she would not mention it.

Tomorrow.

She didn't think she ought to venture back out into the front room again tonight.

Not because she thought he was likely to jump her bones. She thought the revelation of her parentage had pretty much put the lid on that temptation.

It was her own temptation she was concerned about. There was a very large part of her that wished she'd kept her mouth shut and let him get on with his seduction.

The notion shocked her. Poppy Hamilton was not the

sort of girl who entertained lightly the notion of going to bed with a man. The fact of the matter was, she'd never gone to bed with a man. Not even Chad.

He "respected" her too much, he'd told her at the time.

Her cheeks still burned at how gullible she'd been, believing a thing like that.

Still, Chad aside, it was true: she'd never been one for casual sex.

Until now.

She pressed her hands to her cheeks, felt them burn even hotter and knew it had nothing to do with Chad's perfidy. It had everything to do with the idea that she was actually entertaining the notion of making love with Shane Nichols.

"Now who's blushing?" she chided herself.

She wasn't serious about making love with him, was she?

Of course she wasn't.

But he was, hands down, the most tempting man she'd ever met in her life.

Not just the blue eyes and handsome face. It was more than that. More than his narrow-hipped jeans-clad butt, too, even though that had caught her eye right off, the night she'd him at The Barrel. She was something of a connoisseur when it came to an appreciation of a Wrangler-wrapped rear end. But usually her admiration stopped there because the rest of the man was not worth writing home about.

In this case Poppy had let her gaze wander north, expecting to be disappointed, only to find herself catching her breath.

It wasn't just the ubiquitous cowboy hat set atop short midnight-dark hair that caused her throat to constrict and her heart to trip. Nor the sharp nose, high cheekbones and generous mouth. It was all of the above and more. The more being the grin on that mouth, the grooves in his cheeks, and most especially the dancing light in those bright blue eyes.

This man was *alive*.

She'd found it hard to look at anyone else.

All evening long she had watched him. More than once their eyes had met and, embarrassed at her blatant interest in a stranger, Poppy had looked away.

It was a pity, she remembered thinking, that she couldn't find a man like him to take home to her father. But she didn't know him. And she never would.

She never expected to see him again.

But she had.

Once or twice the next day she'd glimpsed him—or thought she had—out of the corner of her eye. Of course Livingston wasn't exactly a metropolis. It was possible to see the same people several times in one day, so she dismissed it. But then tonight at the rehearsal dinner, she'd seen him at the bar.

Once more their gazes had met. This time they'd lingered. Connected.

The charge was almost electric.

It had taken a moment for Poppy to recollect herself and hurry on. She was relieved—but a little disappointed—that when she came back, he was no longer there.

Still, his presence hadn't seemed quite so coincidental, and she wondered if he was as intrigued by her as she was by him.

But she thought it was just wishful thinking when they came out after dinner and she thought she saw him sitting in a truck in the parking lot. It was snowing so hard by then she couldn't be sure.

Forget it, she'd told herself. And she had—until she'd come out of the church and found him waiting for her.

It had seemed right.

Inevitable.

And then he'd approached her, and she'd been shocked, and then dismayed, to discover he thought she was Milly!

She was irritated that he'd wanted to talk about Cash. As far as she was concerned, Cash was responsible for his own life—and problems. If Cash didn't care enough about Milly to stop her from marrying Mike, well, then Milly was better off without him.

Poppy had wanted the dark-haired cowboy to talk to her for herself—because he wanted to talk to *her*.

When he scooped her up and tossed her in his truck, she was amazed. And a little giddy. And scared. Not to mention furious.

But that was before she realized he thought she was Milly.

Then she'd wanted to laugh.

But she couldn't. Not if she wanted Milly's wedding to come off.

If she wanted Milly's wedding to come off, she had to play along.

After all, if he kidnapped the woman he thought was the bride, he wouldn't be able to kidnap the real one, would he?

So she played along.

To help Milly out.

That was all. Wasn't it?

Well, not precisely.

If she got kidnapped, she wouldn't have to meet her

father's candidate for the perfect husband. All week long she'd been trying to figure out how to avoid meeting this paragon at the wedding. She'd never considered getting someone to kidnap her.

But if a gorgeous, well-meaning, slightly mistaken cowboy took it into his head to do so, well, who was she to object?

And then there was Shane himself.

She was still amazed at her reaction to him. After Chad she hadn't let herself react to anyone. She'd wondered sometimes if she still could.

Well, that was one question answered!

But she really wasn't going to go to bed with him, was she?

God, it always seemed to keep coming back to that!

Why? she asked herself. Because, she answered honestly, she really thought she might.

After all, how was she going to know if her father's idea of the perfect man was really perfect if she didn't have anything to compare him to? How was she going to be able to make a responsible decision about her future, if she didn't just once behave irresponsibly?

Not *totally* irresponsibly. Heaven knew she believed in safe sex.

But just once to touch, to caress, to hold. To know a man intimately. She wouldn't expect more than was offered. She knew there would be no long term with a man like Shane Nichols. And why should there be? They barely knew each other....

And as long as she accepted that up front...

In her twenty-five years Poppy had never, ever had a fling. Not just a sexual fling—*any* kind of fling. She'd never taken a week, or even a day, off from being responsible, determined, sane-and-sensible Poppy, Judge Hamilton's daughter.

Either she'd been living up to him or vigilantly fighting to stay independent of him or regretting her foolish mistake with Chad as long as she could remember.

She could never remember being able to relax.

And, God, she wanted to relax.

She wanted to laugh, to smile, to stretch out her arms and breathe deeply and know her father was not standing in the background judging. She wanted to sing and dance and throw snowballs and maybe even roll around in the snow or on this bed with that sexy, blushing cowboy and not think about the right man for the rest of her life.

Just for a day. Maybe two.

She wouldn't ask for more. And then—when they dug out—she would go back to being herself.

She didn't dislike being herself. She didn't dislike her father. She just needed a break. A breather. A time-out.

And then, renewed, she would go back to the fray.

And when she got there, she would try to find the perfect man and have those grandchildren her father desired. And when she did, she would pick a suitable man—one her father would approve of.

As much as she might battle with him, deep down she was his daughter. She valued the same things he did— honesty, loyalty, the courage of one's convictions, the determination to do the right thing and the responsibility to accept the consequences of doing the wrong ones.

Her husband, unlike Chad, would value those things, too.

In the end she would do her father proud—in her way—and they would both be happy as clams.

But in the meantime, she was going practice a little *carpe diem.*

She was going to enjoy these brief days with this wholly unsuitable cowboy God had dropped into her life.

He couldn't sleep.

Of course he couldn't sleep!

How the hell could he possibly sleep when he'd just found out that the woman he'd kidnapped was Hard-Ass Hamilton's daughter?

Shane lay there on the lumpy couch, a spring stabbing him in the back, and wondered whether if he threw himself down on it hard enough he could impale himself and thus end his miserable life.

The way his luck was running lately it seemed unlikely.

Why couldn't he learn to keep his big mouth shut? Why couldn't he learn to be satisfied with a sane, normal life like other men?

Why did he have to go around kidnapping judges' daughters?

Well, he'd only kidnapped one judge's daughter.

So far, he thought gloomily. He was young yet. God only knew how many more he might inadvertently run off with.

He moaned. He twisted. And turned. The spring stabbed him again. It was like sleeping on a bed of nails.

Just punishment, he was sure Mace would have said.

Shane didn't want to think what Hard-Ass Hamilton would say.

His only comfort was that he hadn't taken Poppy across any state lines. At least the old man couldn't give him the death penalty.

Though it might be preferable if he did.

Hamilton was a past master at discovering a guy's Achilles' heel. He seemed to know exactly how to make a guy miserable. God, did he know! Hard-Ass Hamilton had, with malice and justice aforethought, once managed to make Shane more miserable than he'd ever been in his life.

But he'd been a kid then. Giddy and irresponsible and high on beer. It was depressing to realize that he didn't even have any of those excuses now. Thanks to his age, his thumb and the doc's orders, he'd managed to make a complete and utter ass of himself at age thirty-two stone-cold sober.

He'd kidnapped the wrong girl.

And, worse, he'd tried to seduce her!

He thought about getting up and going to the door of the bedroom and tapping on the door and apologizing, saying he'd made a mistake, that he hadn't intended any of it, and that it was another Judge Hamilton he meant.

But why add lying to his growing multitude of sins?

Besides, she'd think he was only doing it because he was afraid of her father.

He *was* afraid of her father.

He could shut his eyes now and see the bushy-browed judge leaning down from the bench and staring straight at him.

"What you need," he'd said in that ponderous gravelly voice of his, "is to start thinking about the consequences of your actions." Pause. "Don't you, Mr. Nichols?"

"Yes, sir."

"When you do these things, you have to expect your chickens to come home to roost, isn't that right, Mr. Nichols?"

"Yes, sir."

Once the judge found out about this latest escapade, Shane thought with a shudder, the chicken would doubtless be winging its way back.

Five

It was an aberration. The product of shock.

In the clear light of day, waking up in the cabin's tiny bedroom after the most wonderful night's sleep, Poppy saw last night's temptation for the foolishness it was.

She wasn't going to do anything stupid like go to bed with a man she hardly knew.

Tempting as it was, It would be a mistake to sleep with Shane Nichols just for the sake of having a "new experience."

Making love ought to be just that—making *love*. She knew that. She accepted it.

But that didn't mean she couldn't enjoy the rest of this unexpected little interlude. It didn't mean she couldn't enjoy getting to know him, exploring the rather amazing attraction she felt for him.

After all, who knew when she might ever get kidnapped by a sexy cowboy again?

"The greatest joy," her mother had told her urgently right before her own death, "is to be open to life. Embrace it. Live every moment."

Good advice, Poppy knew. But most of her life, she didn't have time.

Most of her life Poppy was so busy battling her father's plans for her in order to keep some independence or fending off the men he brought home to meet her, that she couldn't concentrate on enjoying the moment. She always had to keep her guard up and be thinking one step ahead.

She supposed that, even as she embraced the moment, it would be wise to keep her guard up with Shane Nichols. She was relatively certain he wasn't another Chad. But there were other men in the world it wouldn't do to fall in love with.

Rolling stones, for one. Men who were here today, gone tomorrow.

Men like Shane.

So, all right. She would be careful. She would protect her heart. She didn't—wouldn't—have any expectations. Beyond now.

But couldn't she try to enjoy now?

Her father wasn't anywhere near. He didn't even know where she was. He wouldn't be worried about her, either. Not right away. He would just think she'd got cold feet when faced with having to meet his "perfect man."

Let him think it. It was a version of the truth.

A better version than she could have imagined.

And so for now, she resolved, she would enjoy this moment—and this man.

"Good morning!"

The cheerful female voice rocked Shane out of a fitful

sleep. He squinted into the morning light, saw the bright smiling face of Poppy Hamilton looking down at him and groaned.

It had taken him hours to finally fall asleep, and when at last he had, his dreams had been filled with rampaging judges, wide-eyed, dark-haired, drop-dead gorgeous women. And chickens.

He'd told himself it was something he ate.

Now he remembered it was something he'd done.

Deliberately he shut his eyes again. "Whuz good about it?"

"Well, for one thing," Poppy said brightly, "it's still snowing."

She sounded so happy, he had to open his eyes to see if he was dreaming. He couldn't believe she was as pleased as she sounded. But apparently she was, for she was smiling and humming as she pushed back the curtains to the kitchen window and let the soft silvery morning light into the room.

Confused, Shane struggled halfway up, squinting as he tried to focus on what was beyond the frosted pane. What he saw was white. All white. Snow white—and plenty of it.

But he was still surprised she was happy about it.

He looked at her suspiciously. Had her father shown up while he was sleeping? Was the judge going to give him his comeuppance now without benefit of trial—where no one would find his body until spring?

He looked at her warily. "How come you're humming?"

"I'm happy."

"Why?"

"You mean besides getting to spend who knows how

many days stranded in a tiny log cabin with you?'' She smiled at him.

Shane didn't want her smiling at him. Her smile played havoc with the little good sense he had.

"Besides that," he muttered.

She shrugged amiably and kept right on smiling. "I like snow. And I've discovered I like being stranded in the snow. It's a very...freeing... experience."

"You're nuts."

"Probably." But she sounded happy about that, too. She turned away and began scavenging through the cupboards, setting packages on the counter as she did so. "Would you prefer dehydrated scrambled eggs or beef Stroganoff or the remains of the chili?"

As a last meal none of them sounded very appealing.

"I don't care," he said dully.

"Ah, not a morning person? Never mind." She turned back to the foil bags, and picked one. "Let's have the eggs." And, beginning to hum once more, she set about fixing them. "And there's some biscuit mix. Good."

Shane sat where he was. He tried to make his mind work in a calm orderly fashion. He tried to tell himself that things weren't as bad as they seemed, that at any minute the sun would shine, the snow would melt and he could return the judge's daughter, whom he had kidnapped and who was presently humming and smiling and fixing him breakfast.

Yeah, right.

So much for thinking straight.

And anyway, he was distracted by watching her. Despite her parentage, Poppy Hamilton was still the most attractive woman he'd ever seen. And even when his mind knew better, his body didn't.

He liked curvy women, and the sight of her hips when

she bent to get a frying pan out of the cupboard made his hands itch to learn their shape.

Yeah, that's right, compound your sins, he told himself. *See what the judge thinks of that.* He knotted his hands into fists to make them behave and cleared his mind of all such thoughts. It didn't work. He could still see her. He could still hear her humming.

"You always this cheery?" he grumbled.

"Not always. But I had a wonderful night's sleep."

"Lucky you." Shane didn't know which had kept him awake more—the sofa or his memories of the judge.

"I take it you didn't?"

He flexed the taut muscles of his shoulders, trying to get the kinks out. "Not quite. You know what they say—no rest for the weary."

She lifted a brow. "I thought that was wicked?"

"That, too, obviously." He paused, then said awkwardly. "You're, um, being a very good sport about this."

Poppy dumped the egg powder into a bowl. "I told you, I'm enjoying it."

"Why? Because it's—" what had she called it? "—freeing?"

She nodded as she measured out the water and added it to the eggs. "No responsibilities. No demands. Just here and now. And you."

Shane gulped. He scrabbled for his shirt and dragged it on as if it could protect him from the intensity of her gaze. "You aren't going to...get in trouble for missing the wedding?"

"Less than if Milly had missed it," she said cheerfully.

Too true.

Shane finished buttoning his shirt one-handed. "I

don't need any eggs," he said. "I'll go out and start shoveling again."

"Won't do any good. It's still snowing too hard. Why not just relax and enjoy it?"

He looked at her. Didn't she realize?

"Come on," she said. "Sit down and eat. After, I'll wash, you dry and, if you're still that desperate to go shovel, I'll go with you."

She made biscuits, too, while he was taking a shower. They ate the eggs, and she found a jar of jam for the biscuits. But she couldn't get the cap off. Shane didn't know, given that he only had one good hand to work with, if he could, either.

But finally he did by anchoring the jar between his knees and twisting with his right hand.

"Hooray!" Poppy cheered. She beamed at him.

Pleased with his one tiny accomplishment, he grinned back, and felt that electric connection arc between them again. "I'll take my biscuits with me," he said. "It's time I got to shoveling."

The snow was falling almost as hard now as it had been the night before. Poppy wouldn't let him go alone. So they bundled up and Shane wrapped the biscuits in a sack and tucked them into his pocket and, together, they set off.

It took almost half an hour to get to the truck. When they got there he found that all last night's work had gone for naught. The snow was drifted back even higher and now reached above the truck sides to the camper top.

"It's impossible," Poppy said. "Truly."

But Shane tried. He had to try. It was better than being inside that matchbox-size cabin with her. Listening to her hum. Watching her move. Seeing her smile at him.

Aching. Wishing.

He was outside in the cold. In the snow.

Nothing could happen out here.

And nothing did happen until he had to stop, exhausted. Then he turned around to see her helping him.

She had cleared off the truck once more and was now scooping snow away from the door with her hands. She was trying to help, but was actually getting more in her hair and on her eyelashes than anywhere else.

When her eyes met his, she laughed. It was the same wonderful laugh he could remember from the night at The Barrel, and it sent a shaft of desire right through him.

"This is insane!" she said as the wind whipped more snow in her face. "Why are we doing this?" She laughed again and tossed her head. Her hair brushed his cheek.

"Because..." his voice caught in his throat.

"Because?"

"Because if we don't, I might do this." And he dropped the shovel and hauled her into his arms and kissed her.

He couldn't help himself. He'd been tempted too long. His desire was too strong. His will was too weak. His mind too feeble.

Nothing made sense anymore—except kissing Poppy.

She was sweet.

She was gentle.

She was like one of her flowers—delicate and yielding—as gradually her lips softened and parted and she opened her mouth to him, welcomed him in.

She didn't seize or plunder or demand like other girls he'd known, determined to show him how eager she was, how desperately ready she was to share herself with him.

She didn't insist.

But she didn't resist, either.

And thank God for that, because Shane needed this kiss like he never remembered needing anything in his life.

He tried to tell himself it was because he'd been without a woman so long, that any woman's lips would have excited him the way Poppy's did, that the sense of connectedness, of rightness that he felt when his lips were touching hers wasn't unusual at all.

But he wasn't capable of that much rational thought in a lifetime, let alone when his hormones were singing the ''Hallelujah Chorus'' and his body had a good start on a Sousa march.

He loved the feel of her mouth beneath his. After his initial desperation, he relaxed, letting nature take its course. And when it did, her lips parted and her breath mingled with his. He couldn't help his tongue finding hers, tasting hers. He couldn't stop the gentle probing, couldn't fight the equally tender touch of her tongue tangling with his in return.

It made him ache with wanting more of her. It made him tremble with needing all of her. *All of her!*

His body pressed closer, fitted itself to hers, despite the bulk of their clothing. And it felt right. It did.

Their mouths seemed made for each other's. Their bodies, too, seemed somehow to fit. Her hair blew around them. The snow melted on them. Neither one of them noticed.

Poppy was kissing him with as much fervor as he was kissing her.

And that, perhaps, is what woke him up. It scared

him—the intensity of her response. It was pure and undiluted. There was no artifice. No teasing. No playing games.

Poppy wasn't dallying with him.

He didn't dare dally with her.

And that was when he finally managed to stumble back and break off the kiss.

Shaking, he wiped a hand down his face. It was freezing, and he was sweating. His heart was hammering. Poppy looked stunned.

"I'm sorry," Shane said hoarsely. "I shouldn't have...I didn't mean...I never—"

But whatever he tried to say only seemed to make her look worse. Her expression went from stunned to stricken.

She turned and scrabbled up the side of the ditch, then onto the road. Floundering through the snow, she began to run.

He cursed under his breath and began to run after her. He slipped, fell, caught himself on his bad hand and winced. Then he stumbled to his feet again and lurched after her.

"Poppy! Poppy, damn it! Wait!"

She had a head start now. He could barely see her through the wind-whipped snow. His heart was slamming against the wall of his chest. His blood pounded in his ears as he tripped and staggered through the drifts. "Poppy!"

He was gasping by the time he finally caught up with her.

She didn't stop. Didn't look at him.

He grabbed her arm and jerked her around. "Don't run off like that! Don't *ever* run off like that! You could get lost! You could die out here alone!"

"Why would you care?" she said crossly, wrenching her arm out of his grasp and turning to continue plowing through the snow.

"You're my responsibility. You—"

"I absolve you of all responsibility." She still didn't look at him.

He stumbled alongside her, still gulping air. "You... can't."

Her steps hesitated. "Can't? Why not?"

"Code of...ethics. Not the way it's done. Kidnapee is always...kidnapper's responsibility."

She stopped then and looked at him closely. They were close together again. Very close. Too close. He took a step back. But he let a grin touch his mouth and he never took his eyes off hers.

Poppy shook her head. Her shoulders slumped. A faint, weary smile touched her lips. "You are crazy. You know that?"

"I know." *Oh, God, did he ever!*

They kept looking at each other still. All the desire was still there. He could see it in her eyes. He could feel it inside him. But he couldn't let it happen. And not just because of the judge, either.

He could hurt this woman. He could see it in her eyes. But he wouldn't. He would never knowingly hurt anyone. Especially her.

He shook his head. "No," he said softly.

The light dimmed in Poppy's eyes. She looked away. She started to move again, but she wasn't running now, just plodding steadily.

Shane slipped his hand in the crook of her arm and wondered if she would resist. She stiffened, but she didn't pull away. She just walked. He matched his stride to hers.

Her coat brushed his as they walked, her arm jostled against his side, her hair blew in his face. A faint scent of springtime assailed him.

He tried not to notice. He told himself that it was just like walking an old lady across the street, then jeered. When had he ever walked any old ladies across a street? And what old lady wore a soft flowery scent that, even in the midst of a damn blizzard, could drive a man insane.

It took forever to get to the cabin.

It didn't take nearly long enough.

When they got there, Shane let go of her arm and turned to go back.

"Don't," Poppy said.

"Got to."

"Why?"

"I can't stay here."

"Why?"

"You know why."

They stared at each other.

Then she shook her head. "I don't. Or," she added after a moment's reflection, "maybe I do." She smiled a little bitterly. "I'm...the wrong girl."

"You're not," Shane said at once. "Not at all. It's just...I wish..." He shook his head. There was no point. No wish could make it happen. "You're not the wrong girl. I'm just...the wrong man for you."

Six

It's what you wanted, after all, wasn't it? Poppy asked herself, her fingers at her lips even as she watched him go.

He was going to the barn, at least. Not back to the truck.

"I'll be there if you need me," he'd said over his shoulder, and now she could see that he was almost there.

It felt like he was still here. She could still feel his mouth on hers...what she'd wanted.

A kiss from an unsuitable man. A break from routine. A momentary fling. A lark.

What she'd wanted. Not what she'd got.

What she got was hunger and desperation and passion and need all rolled into one mind-blowing, earth-shaking, emotion-numbing kiss.

What she got was so far removed from the dutiful

pecks that Chad used to give her that she felt as if she'd entered a whole new universe.

Slowly, still thinking about that, she shut the cabin door and leaned against it. She needed it to shore her up.

She remembered Milly saying that sometimes when Cash kissed her she completely forgot who she was.

Poppy had never been able to imagine for one instant forgetting she was Georgia Winthrop Hamilton, daughter of the estimable judge.

Now she could.

She'd only thought of the man with his lips on hers. Had thought only of how right it felt, how good, how wonderful.

And she knew that if Shane hadn't pulled back she would be kissing him still.

Or doing other things with him, wild, wicked, wonderful things that the daughter of Judge George Hamilton would never do if she remembered who she was!

It was as well he'd left, Poppy told herself. She needed space, too. And time.

And an ounce of common sense.

She would find it. *Of course* she would find it. She was her father's daughter. And then she would be glad he'd had the sense to put two doors and a blizzard between them.

But for the rest of the day, even while she was looking for that bit of common sense, she kept wishing he would come back.

It was his punishment, Shane decided.

It was just retribution for meddling in other people's business, breaking the law, commandeering a woman—

even the wrong one, *especially the wrong one*—a woman he had no right to.

This time, though, it wasn't his mom or dad or even, heaven help him, Judge Hamilton, dishing out the punishment. It was God telling him he'd overstepped the bounds.

He shouldn't have been surprised. He couldn't remember ever getting away with anything in his entire life. Why should he expect things to be any different now?

It was just, in this case, he seemed to be being dealt with by a higher court. The *highest* court.

He supposed there was a bright side. God seemed to go a little easier on him than Judge Hamilton or his father ever had.

He spent most of the day in the barn, figuring all this out, coming to terms with it—with Poppy Hamilton.

And he accepted it. What else could he do?

There wasn't a court of appeals in a thing like this. And even if there were, no one and nothing—not even his own hormones—would be on his side.

He'd just have to tough it out. Resist. Be noble.

That had to be the message. Why else would God have stranded him in a cabin with the one woman on earth he didn't dare touch?

If God had wanted him to make love to Poppy Hamilton, He sure wouldn't have given her a father like the judge!

"I got the picture," Shane told God—and the owl sitting in the rafters of the barn. "I don't like it, but I'll go along with it."

He waited. All was silent.

Was he expecting maybe God to say what a good boy he was? Hell was likely to freeze over first.

"Try not to make this snow last forever, though, will You?" he added after a moment. "You know better than anyone about me and willpower."

The owl spread its wings and fluttered on its perch. Then it looked down at him and hooted.

Swell. God was a ventriloquist.

Something that smelled wonderful was simmering on the stove when he let himself back into the cabin. It was early evening and the snow was still falling, and there would be hours to go before he could sleep alone on his bed of nails that passed for a couch.

But he was ready. He was prepared to be polite, to help cook supper, to be polite, to read a book or stare at the fire, to make small talk. To be polite.

Poppy was sitting by the fire reading a book. She looked up when he came in and watched as he shed his jacket and boots. She looked at him warily. She didn't speak.

He didn't either, for a moment. Then he turned to her and said, "Whatever you cooked smells fantastic."

She brightened. The worried expression left her face. "You're hungry?"

"Starved." And the moment he said it, he realized how true it was. The rehydrated eggs had been a long time ago. And it had been hours since he'd eaten the biscuits he'd stowed in his pocket.

"Come and eat," Poppy suggested, getting up and moving to the stove. She had already set the table. It reminded him of when Mace and Jenny were living here. It looked homey. Comfortable. Inviting.

More punishment.

But oddly, it didn't feel like punishment. It felt… right.

He helped her dish up. She'd made the Stroganoff and served it over rice. She apologized for the lack of fresh vegetables like it was her fault.

"I think I'll survive," Shane said, smiling slightly. "I'm more of a meat and potatoes man, anyway."

"No potatoes, either," she said sadly.

"I like rice." He sat down across from her at the table and picked up his fork.

For a while they both ate in silence. But the silence didn't seem quite so tension charged this time.

Then Poppy said, "I wonder how the wedding went."

"Fine, probably," Shane replied. "What could go wrong?" He gave her a wry smile.

She smiled back. "I'm glad I wasn't there."

He looked up, surprised. "Why?"

She hesitated. "My father was coming, and he was bringing me his idea of my perfect husband."

Shane gaped. He couldn't imagine. He still had a hard enough time trying to imagine old Hard—old Judge Hamilton being Poppy's father. He really couldn't bend his mind around the notion of the judge on the lookout for a husband.

"He'd have to be a damn paragon," he muttered now.

Poppy nodded. "I'm afraid he is."

"And he expected you to just...marry this guy?" He couldn't quite swallow that, either.

"My father, as you might guess, has had a lot of expectations for me over the years. Like I was going to go to Yale. And I didn't. Like I was going to be a lawyer. And I'm not. Finding me the perfect husband is his latest scheme for getting my life on what he considers the 'right track.' He was going to introduce us. See if we...fit. But yes, ultimately that's what it would amount to."

"And he thinks he ought to be able to do that?" Shane was outraged. He knew how much he hated Jenny trying to find women who would settle him down. Damn it, he didn't *want* to settle down! He didn't think anybody ought to be forced.

"It's just the way he is. And he thinks I need a husband."

"Why?"

"Because I'm twenty-five years old and single," she said lightly. "And he wants to be a grandfather."

Shane rolled his eyes at the thought of the judge as a grandfather. He'd sure as shooting make his grandkids toe the line.

"It's not just that, though, either," Poppy said. "He really thinks he's helping me. He knows I want one. A husband. And a family, I mean." She looked wistful as she spoke. A little sad.

"You're still young," Shane said hastily. "Life hasn't exactly passed you by."

"No." But she didn't sound certain. She poked at her Stroganoff with her fork.

"And he might have the right one," he went on. "He'd have pretty high standards, I reckon."

"Oh, yes."

"So...um, what do you figure he's going to say when he, um...finds out about...this?"

Poppy looked up, curious. "This?"

"Your not showing up at the wedding. Your...getting, er...commandeered. I sort of reckon he'll be coming after me with an arrest warrant." Shane joked, but he didn't exactly think it was funny.

"He might," Poppy said, which didn't help his appetite any. "But I don't plan to tell him."

Shane stared. "You don't?"

"Not unless you want me to."

He shook his head violently. "Not really," he said, trying for as much blasé indifference as he could manage.

Poppy grinned. "Somehow I got the feeling you wouldn't."

Shane rubbed a hand against the back of his neck. "Yeah, well, I don't guess he thinks very highly of me. And somehow I don't think my kidnapping his kid would improve his impression."

"So it's our secret," Poppy said. She slanted him a glance. "Yes?"

Their eyes met. Shane nodded and breathed just a little easier. "Yes."

Dinner lasted hours. It seemed like minutes.

It wasn't the food; though it was far better than Shane expected.

It was the conversation. The increasingly easy give and take that seemed to be developing between them.

"I'm not going to lie to him," Poppy said about telling her father. "I'm going to say I went to the mountains with a friend. We are friends, aren't we?"

Shane nodded slowly. Friends?

"Yeah," he said. "We're friends."

Their eyes met, locked. Something strong and elemental arced between them. Friendship?

Whatever happened to divine punishment?

"Tell me more," Poppy said, "about what happened to your thumb."

So he did. He told her about the accident—the freakish chain of events that had started with him helping out a friend, which had led to him losing his thumb, having the good sense to grab it, and the good fortune to get it sewn back on.

She was the only person besides his rodeo buddies and his blood-thirsty nephews who listened avidly to the whole grisly story without making a face or covering their ears.

She didn't say, "If you'd ever once think about the consequences of what you decide to do, you'd be more careful what you got into," which is what Jenny had said to him.

She didn't say, "Trust you," like Mace had said with a knowing shake of his head.

She didn't say, "I've heard of accident prone, but you take the cake," which is what Taggart had said.

Poppy said, "What a terrific friend you are! I don't know many people who'd have had the presence of mind to do what you did, looking for your thumb and picking it up instead of panicking."

And Shane basked in her approval. And then he told her about the almost clinical detachment he'd felt—as if the accident had happened to somebody else. And that what had happened didn't really hit home until he woke up after the surgery. "By then," he said, "I was flat on my back, and no one noticed I'd passed out. They thought I was sleeping!"

Poppy giggled delightedly.

And Shane gave a self-deprecating laugh. "That's me. Capable. Unflappable under duress. Always on the ball."

"And modest. Don't forget modest." Poppy grinned. She got up and poured them each another cup of coffee.

Shane grinned, too, unnettled by her gentle teasing. It didn't have the bite that Mace's always had. Instead of flying off the handle or fighting back as he always did with his brother, he more or less basked in hers. He stretched and flexed his shoulders, thought about getting up and decided not to.

Usually he didn't linger after a meal. Usually he was restless, antsy, glancing at his watch and tapping his feet and raring to go. Not tonight.

Of course there was nowhere to go—not with three feet of snow outside.

But it was more than that.

He didn't *want* to go anywhere else. He didn't want to *be* anywhere else. He wanted to be here.

With Poppy.

He watched as she added a little milk to his coffee, not much, just as much as she'd seen him add earlier. But he liked that she'd paid attention. Jenny always added too much, and Mace always made a face and said, "What's the matter, kid, can't you drink your coffee straight?"

Poppy handed him the mug and smiled at him.

He took it and smiled back. Something dangerously like contentment stole through him, catching him unawares.

He felt a prickle of worry and promptly dismissed it. There would be time enough to worry about the feelings he was experiencing.

Right now, he just wanted to experience them. Shane was a man who lived for the moment. He'd long ago realized that it was all there was.

The past was over. The future was worrisome, but happily vague. This was the best moment he'd had in quite some time. He wasn't about to second-guess it.

Poppy tipped her head and regarded him through her lashes, "I bet you always wanted to ride bulls. Didn't you? From the first time you saw one ridden, I bet."

She was right. He didn't know how she knew that, but she did.

Most people couldn't understand why he rode. They had a hard time fathoming what made a man pit his all against a ton of bovine nastiness when he didn't have to.

Shane couldn't seem to explain that he *did* have to, that from the very first time he'd seen a bull ride at the Wilsall rodeo when he was four, he'd had to ride, too.

What was for others a risk well beyond the normal bounds of reason, was for him an elemental challenge that could not be ignored.

Maybe it was because, even at that early age, he'd always felt so much unbridled energy himself. He'd needed to direct it at something so big, so ferocious, so untamed, in order to harness it…to find a purpose for it.

"I did," he said now. "It's who I am."

And Poppy nodded. "Yes. I understand."

He supposed she did—she who was a florist instead of a lawyer. She who had grown up fighting every day just to be herself. In fact, he thought she might understand better than anyone he'd ever met.

"It's the challenge," he told her. "Doing my best. Against the odds. And living with the outcome. Whatever it is."

"Yes." She nodded. "Yes."

He told her about Dusty, a particularly nasty one-horned Brangus who seemed to particularly have it in for him. "Every time I rode him, he tried something new, something wicked. It was like he sat up late plannin' his moves!"

He told her about Sterling Silver, a huge white Brahma, the biggest bull he'd ever ridden. "Like sittin' on a sofa,'' he said. ''One that could toss you to the moon.''

He told her about Skeezix, that mean little sunfishing bull from New Mexico, and Doberman, so called because he didn't just jab you and stomp you and buck you. ''He tried to take a bite out of you, too.''

''You remember them all?''

''Damn near. Only ones I don't are the ones that concussed me.'' He sighed and tipped back in his chair, cradling his mug in his good hand. He looked at the cast on his other one. It covered this miracle of modern medicine—a reattached thumb. And he wondered, not for the first time, what would happen if it couldn't face the rigors of his profession.

''Good as new?'' he remembered his doctor saying when Shane had pressed him for a prognosis. ''We don't know, do we? We can only hope.''

He thought about how it was hard some days to unbend all the joints and stretch out all the muscles in his entire body. The effects of fourteen years on the bulls was cumulative. He knew that. But he didn't know what to do about it—or instead of it. And now there was his thumb.

His thumb was the tip of the iceberg that was his fear.

''I don't know what I'll do,' he said, staring down into the mug, ''if…when…I can't ride anymore.''

It was the first time he'd spoken the words out loud; the first time he'd articulated the terror of the emptiness he would be facing when bull riding—the one thing that gave his life focus, purpose and meaning—was no longer there.

Poppy didn't answer.

She sat quietly, watched him sympathetically over the top of the coffee mug. She didn't offer any glib suggestions. She didn't dismiss his fear or even try to minimize it.

She held his gaze and shared it as she shared the bleakness in his voice and the sentiment it expressed.

"What else do you love?" she asked him at last.

He shook his head. What else *did* he love?

"What else makes it worthwhile getting up every morning?"

He didn't know the answer to that, either. Poppy stirred her coffee and looked away toward the fire in the fireplace. "It's like a death, isn't it?"

He shot her a quizzical look.

"When my mother died, I felt lost. Bereft. I knew I was going to lose her. She'd been sick for a couple of years. Inside, I knew the day was going to come when she wouldn't be there anymore. But even so, I wasn't prepared. I was devastated. And sick. And I didn't see how I was going to go on. Everything felt so empty."

Shane had been to the edge of that abyss himself when his own parents had died, but he'd barely allowed himself to look over. Instead he'd left Mace to deal with it, and he'd flung himself into the grind—and the salvation—of going down the road.

But when he could no longer go... When he had to stop and look around, to take stock, to face the future... When the bull riding was gone...

Yes, he saw what she meant.

"It took me some time," Poppy said softly, her gaze dropping to focus on the mug in her hands. "Some groping. Some just plain muddling through, doing what had to be done. So I started doing it. And that's when I began to understand how much I loved flowers. Tending them, spending time with them, nurturing them, caring for them. So that's what I did. I focused on them. They got me through it.''

She raised her head and looked at him, her eyes gentle, understanding. ''You'll find something like that. I don't know what it will be, but you'll find something or you'll recognize something that was there all along. And that will be the start and you'll be all right.'' She reached out and took his hand, folding his callused, beat-up fingers inside hers. ''I know you will.''

Shane didn't move. Just sat there. Let the warmth from her hand seep into his. Let her comfort seep into him.

It was the oddest, least likely situation in the world. The kidnapper and the kidnappee. The bull rider and the flower girl. Had God's punishment become God's blessing?

Who was he to question it?

Not just that. This—the first serious conversation with a woman other than his sister-in-law—he'd ever had in his life.

He guessed Poppy was right. Someday he would find that something else she was talking about. And he would survive not being able to ride anymore. And the future would hold more joy and less of the emptiness it now promised. Someday…

But for now all he had was today.

Strangely, it was enough.

Seven

That night his bed of nails didn't seem so bad.

Granted, he'd have rather spent it with Poppy. But he slept all right on the sofa. There were no dreams of judges. And the vague bottomless feeling that he got whenever he contemplated the future didn't seem quite so intense.

He lay on the sofa and watched the snow fall and murmured, "Keep it up."

Oddly, this time God seemed to listen.

At least when he awoke in the morning, the snow was still coming down. The world was whiter than ever. He should have been worried. He supposed in some part of his brain—the small, sensible part he so rarely used—he *was* worried.

But mostly, as he looked at the window at the growing drifts and the white sky, he felt the quiet burn of contentment.

He wanted another day here.

With Poppy.

She might not be Milly. But as far as he was concerned, she was better than Milly. She might be Judge Hamilton's daughter, but the judge didn't matter. He was over the hills and far away.

Only Poppy was here.

And Shane was pleased. He liked her. He liked her determination and her gentleness. He liked her stubbornness and her understanding. He liked her smiles and her fiery hazel eyes. He liked whatever this was that had begun to develop between them.

He knew it wasn't going to last. He didn't expect it to. Hell, when had anything in his life lasted longer than eight seconds? But however long it lasted, he was going to take advantage of it.

And interestingly, too, especially after the passion with which they had kissed, his desire to stay here with her had nothing to do with sex.

She was Hard-Ass Hamilton's daughter, after all. He would be crazy to even think about having sex with her.

Well, maybe he could think about it—fantasize a little, imagine what it would be like to have her naked beneath him, to feel her silky skin rubbing against his, to—

He groaned.

No, he couldn't even think about it.

But he could think about the rest of it. It was a little like a game of pretend. Playing house.

Not the sort of house he'd been forced into playing with Taggart's bossy sister Erin when they were little and their big brothers had ditched them, telling them they were "too little" to play the games the big kids played.

Playing house with Erin had almost always ended with him punching her, and her punching him back, and their mothers dragging them apart, and him getting swatted for picking on a girl.

He wondered if Poppy, like Erin, had punched back when she was little. Probably. He grinned. He wondered what she'd been like as a little girl.

"What were you like as a little girl?" he asked her later that afternoon.

They were standing in the front yard. He had just finished digging a path to the gate. It was more of an exercise in futility than usefulness. But it kept him busy. And Poppy worked along with him. And while they worked, they talked.

"What was I like?" she echoed.

He nodded, leaning on the shovel and watching her as she bent and scooped up handfuls of snow. "Yeah. As a little girl."

"Like this," Poppy said, smiling—and she hit him with a snowball in the chest.

"Hey!"

But Poppy scooped another handful and tossed it after the first. A guy could only take so much provocation. He could only tell himself that he was an adult and ought to behave like one for just so long.

"Whoa," Shane said, as the second snowball slid down the front of his jacket. "You are askin' for it."

"You wanted to know," Poppy said and, laughing, she stuck out her tongue at him.

All the electricity in the world seemed to sing in that moment.

"Right." A slow smile dawned on Shane's face. He knew an invitation when he saw—and felt—one.

He scooped up snow in his good hand and with a great deal of joy went after Poppy Hamilton.

It was an act of blatant provocation, and Poppy knew it.

She couldn't help it. She hadn't been able to sleep all night for thinking about Shane Nichols and seeing his beautiful blue eyes and remembering the way his lips felt on hers. She wanted to see more, feel more, know more.

And so she threw the snowball.

She knew what would happen—what she *wanted* to happen. For Shane to pick up the gauntlet she'd thrown down. For Shane to stoop and pick up a handful of snow and come after her.

Poppy shrieked. She ran.

But not fast. And not far.

Just around the corner of the house. Then she bent to gather more snow into a ball, but she didn't get up quickly enough.

And that was where he caught her.

The snowballs came first, lobbed to land in her hair, tossed gently to splatter against her back. And when she turned, laughing, and threw the one she'd made, it caught him square in the jaw.

"Oh, dear!" She turned and started to run again.

Three long strides and he grabbed her. Tackled her.

Down they went in the snow, Poppy laughing and kicking, Shane rolling over, so that when they came to rest, she was on top and he lay looking up at her.

Her breath came in gasps, in giggles. His came in desperate gulps. Their eyes locked.

And the world seemed to stop.

The moment crystallized. All her senses sharpened.

Shane's eyes seemed deeper, bluer. His expression more urgent. His body taut. Aroused.

And yet he made no move. He held himself absolutely, perfectly still. Only his eyes moved, watching hers.

As if the future was up to her.

Her own body trembled. Not with the cold, though the snow slid down the back of her neck and that caught between their bodies melted there. No, she trembled with heat, and warmth and need.

The need to be close. The need to touch.

"Shane?" Her voice was barely more than a whisper.

He answered only with his eyes. He needed it, too.

She got off him. She held out a hand to him, pulled him to his feet, wrapped his fingers in hers, and wouldn't let go. He wrapped an arm around her shoulders and drew her hard against him.

Together, arms around each other they walked back to the house.

Only when they were inside, did he speak. He shut the door and leaned against it and looked right at her.

It was her chance to smile, to say something light and clever, to defuse the situation.

But she couldn't. Wouldn't.

Because somehow in the space of two days, she had fallen in love with him.

It was insane, and she knew it. It was foolish, and she knew that, too.

She had promised herself that she could enjoy these days—these moments—with him and still walk away, because God knew—and she knew—that was what Shane intended to do.

She *had* enjoyed them, more than enjoyed them. That

was the trouble. She had found a man she could talk to, and listen to, and laugh with and play with—and love.

She didn't know why she felt so strongly that they were soul mates. They were as different as a brash, showy amaryllis from a sweet backyard violet. And yet they connected, too.

She wanted to know the fullness of that connection.

She would let him go when she had to.

But once...just once...she had to know.

She slipped her jacket off, then stepped toward him and lifted her hands to his chest. Slowly, carefully, she drew the zipper of his coat down.

He didn't move, except to swallow. But as she slid her hands inside, she could feel his heart pound. The coat undone, she slipped it off his shoulders and dropped it on a chair. Then she put her hands back on his chest, touched the buttons of his shirt and looked deeply into his eyes.

"Poppy?"

Her mouth curved. She touched his cheek. She nodded. "Yes."

She took him with her into the bedroom. She lay with him on the bed. She wrapped her arms around him and savored the feel of his arms around her. She was beneath him this time and looked up to see the serious, intent look on his face.

"Poppy?" he said again.

And again she said, "Yes," and slid her fingers up into his hair.

He bent his head and, slowly and deliberately, Shane touched his mouth to hers.

It was as if every moment of her life so far had been spent merely waiting, as if life hadn't really started until now.

So this is what it's all about, she found herself thinking, when she managed to think at all.

No wonder Milly had looked so dazed and starry-eyed whenever she'd come back from a date with Cash. No wonder she'd been distracted, distant, barely deigning to speak at all.

How could you, Poppy wondered, when you'd just been kissed like this?

But it wasn't just kissing. It was touching. It was the feel of his callused fingers lifting the hem of her sweater and skimming lightly over her heated skin. It was the heavy weight of his body pressed hard into hers, proof of his attraction to her, a testament to his desire.

"If you're gonna stop me, stop me now," Shane said as he fumbled the sweater up and bent his head to lay moist kisses on her abdomen, making her squirm and shiver.

And Poppy said, "No." She couldn't have stopped him. She couldn't have stopped herself. She let her fingers rove over the soft short hair that capped his head. She traced the curve of his ears and then clenched her fingers at his nape when he pressed a kiss right above the button of her jeans.

He lifted his head, looked at her. His expression was a combination of need and desire and the agony of indecision. "I shouldn't—" he muttered.

"You should." She loosed her fingers and touched his cheek with one. "We should. Please."

She saw him swallow, felt something like a shudder run through him. He shut his eyes briefly, then opened them and looked straight at her once again. She thought she could drown in the deep blue of his eyes.

Then, "Whatever you say, Ms. Hamilton," he said.

She knew the words were meant to come out in a soft,

lazy drawl. They didn't. They were ragged and intense. They sounded the way she felt. She grasped his shoulders and tried to pull him up against her. Without his willingness, she couldn't have managed.

But he was willing. He was ever so willing.

Poppy didn't stop to think about the consequences. Whatever they turned out to be, she would handle them. Whatever they were, they would be a small price to pay for this—for his loving her.

She supposed Shane might call what happened between them nothing more than a mutual sharing of pleasure. She supposed he might call it "having sex" or "going to bed" or simply "doing it."

But if he did, he would be wrong.

He made love to her.

She felt it in the gentleness of his hands, in their soft touch, in the unsteady tremor of his fingers as they caressed her heated flesh. She saw it in his eyes, in the way they roved over her body slowly, learning its valleys and hills and memorizing each one. She heard it in his quick eager breath, in the urgent sound he made at the back of his throat as he stripped her shirt over her head. She tasted it in his ever more insistent kisses.

And she loved him, too.

Her father would despair of her. In her saner moments—presuming she ever had any again—she would most likely despair of herself.

But not now.

Now she didn't despair, or think. She simply loved.

She gave of herself. She'd heard the pain in his voice last night. She'd seen the fear in his eyes, the hopelessness he felt when confronting an unknown future. She remembered that fear; she empathized with those feel-

ings. As she'd told him, they were so much like her own
feelings when she'd faced the world without her mother.

She'd wanted reassurance then, someone to share
with. Someone to take her in his arms and tell her she
wasn't alone.

She'd had her father. And her flowers.

Shane had nothing. No one.

But her.

And so she loved him. Not just because she was there.
But because she wanted to.

And after a moment's pause, when he seemed to give
her one last chance to call a halt, which she did not take,
he nodded his head, the way Poppy imagined he would
nod his head before he began a bull ride.

It was the moment of commitment. The moment of
no return.

She was already there.

They moved together, with purpose now, not desperation. Their movements as they shed their clothing and
touched each other's bare flesh were eager, their urgency
real. But there was nothing frantic about their coupling.

It was passionate. It was intense. It was deep.

And as he moved above her, parted her, entered
her—and she welcomed him—it was the most real expression of love she'd ever known.

The pain of it was lost in the wonder of the moment.

On her.

Not on him.

She felt him tense, halt. Curse.

The top of his head dropped to rest against her breasts.
He heaved a breath, held himself rigid. Refused to move.

Poppy, tense, too, from the sudden pain she'd felt and
the shattering feelings that accompanied it—*him!*—

didn't move, either, for a long moment. But her body did. It eased, softened, accommodated itself to him.

She sighed. Then breathed again. Slowly. Carefully. Then more deeply, fully. The pain was gone. The fullness remained. She settled, wrapped her arms around him, drew him further in.

A breath hissed out of him. "Poppy!" He started to pull away.

She held him fast. "Come to me."

"I already did," he said through his teeth. But he hadn't yet. Not fully. She knew that, knew he was still trembling. Shaking with the effort not to press harder, to move quicker, to ease his need in her.

"No." She shook her head. "You haven't. Not yet. Come to me."

"You're a virgin!"

"Was a virgin," she corrected him softly.

He shut his eyes and cursed again under his breath. "You shouldn't have! *We* shouldn't have!"

She lifted a hand away from his sweat-slick back and touched his face, tipped it up, made him look at her. "I wanted this," she told him gently.

"Why?" His voice was anguished. He still didn't move.

"I wanted...I want...you."

The words were soft, simple. Honest. And they broke the only control he had left.

He dropped his head again. A shudder ran through him. And then he began to move.

He was an urgent lover, but at the same time, a gentle one. She knew he craved his own release. She could feel how tight a rein he kept on himself, how hard he worked to hold himself back—to share, to give, to love her the way she needed to be loved.

She wasn't surprised.

It was the kind of man he was. Impulsive. But never selfish. Everything she knew about Shane Nichols told her that. He did what he did not for himself, but for others.

And his loving her was no different.

She tried to love him the same way. She wasn't as skilled as he. She wasn't as experienced. But she seemed to know instinctively how to fit her body to his, how to move with him, how to wrap him in the safety of her arms and her body and bring him the comfort, the release—the love—he needed so much.

And she must have done something right, because his movements became more urgent, his trembling more intense. She felt his need build and build until finally he shattered within her.

And as she held him close, Poppy felt her body tighten, tighten, tighten and then ripplingly release around him. And then she shattered, too.

Broken, yet whole. Splintered, yet somehow forged anew and stronger than she'd ever felt before. She kissed his ear, his jaw, his cheek, the side of his nose, his mouth.

"Thank you," she whispered. "That was beautiful."

He sucked in an unsteady breath. "I'm the one ought to be thanking you." He rolled off, but not away. Propping his head on his hand, he lay quietly, looking at her. He didn't speak. He didn't seem to know what to say.

Poppy didn't, either. Her heart was full. Her mind spun. She felt glorious and bereft at the same time. She had experienced a love, a closeness, a sharing that she'd never felt before. She'd never felt anything more wonderful.

And she was never going to feel it again.

You knew that, she told herself.

And, of course, she had. *You said you'd deal with the consequences, whatever they were,* she reminded herself.

And she knew she would.

But to know such intimacy, to have experienced it and yet to realize it wouldn't last, well, it hurt.

She wished...*wished....*

Something of what she was feeling must have shown in her face for Shane touched her arm. "Are you... okay?"

Poppy forced a smile. "I'm fine," she lied.

"I hurt you."

She shook her head. "No."

Not the way he meant. Not the way that he was going to hurt her when the snow stopped and they left the cabin—and each other—to go their separate ways.

She rolled onto her side, facing him, cradling her head in the crook of her arm and smiled at him again. This time it wasn't so hard. "You didn't hurt me," she told him. "You loved me."

He blinked. But he didn't at once look away. He seemed to consider her words, to weigh them.

And then he, too, smiled. It was a sad smile. Wistful almost. Then he blinked again, several times rapidly, and rolled onto his back to stare up at the ceiling. She saw him swallow.

" wish I could," he said.

So much for restraint.

Had he ever really expected he'd be able to resist the temptation that was Poppy Hamilton?

Even knowing who her father was, had he, Shane Nichols, ever actually believed that he'd be able to do the honorable thing, the *right* thing, and keep his jeans zipped and his hands off her?

Well, he'd hoped.

Sort of.

But not enough, obviously. And now he had that on his conscience as well.

It was a good thing his conscience was used to bearing up under heavy loads, he thought morosely as he studied the woman sleeping beside him.

He wasn't on the sofa tonight.

He would have gone back there again if she'd wanted him to, but she didn't. She wanted him to stay, wanted to sleep with him.

He stayed. He wasn't sleeping.

He was lying there thinking. Aching. Wishing.

He'd wanted sex. He'd thought that was what he was after. And he'd got it.

And more.

So much more he couldn't quite fathom it even yet. He'd been given unconditional love. Poppy Hamilton's virginity. And more than that even. Her heart and soul.

He knew it. He saw it in her eyes, felt it in her touch. Knew what was happening and was powerless to stop it. Didn't *want* to stop it. He only wanted her.

And he tried to give her what he could of himself in return.

It wasn't much. It wasn't enough.

Nothing he had would ever be enough for her.

Maybe she *wouldn't* tell her father about him kidnapping her. Maybe he would get off scot-free. Maybe no one would ever know what had happened, except the two of them.

And maybe, if he hadn't made love with her, he could have forgotten it himself in time.

Not now.

Now he would carry with him the memories of the sweetest, most beautiful lovemaking he'd ever shared. Now he would move on and know that the best was behind him. Now he would go to his grave carrying the impression of Poppy Hamilton's smiling face in his heart.

The judge would say it served him right.

They awoke to sunshine, snow melt and Taggart Jones clumping up the front steps.

"Shane? You here? Hello!"

Poppy's eyes snapped open wide. "Who's that?"

Shane, muttering swear words, stumbled out of bed and scrabbled for his jeans. "Taggart. Guy who owns the cabin. Prob'ly up checking the herd and saw the truck. 'M here," he yelled back. "Hold your horses!"

He threw Poppy the shirt she'd shed during their lovemaking, then he stepped into his jeans and yanked them up and hurried to open the door.

"Saw your truck in the ditch when I was makin' a circle," Taggart said when Shane opened the door. "You okay?"

"Fine." Shane got the jeans zipped, but gave up on the button and left his shirt hanging open. "Just...sleeping in. I tried digging out a couple of times. Couldn't make it. Got pretty tired."

"I guess. What the hell were you doin' up here?"

"Drivin' around."

"In a blizzard?"

Shane hunched his shoulders. "You've never done a stupid thing in your life?"

"One or two," Taggart said. He frowned at the sound of bedsprings in the other room. "Someone else here?"

A light seemed to dawn in his head. He looked at Shane, his expression far less puzzled now. He grinned.

Shane scowled. "None of your business."

A corner of Taggart's mouth lifted. "Not as long as she's here of her own free will."

Shane felt his cheeks warm, but he managed an indignant look. "You reckon I kidnapped someone?"

Taggart laughed. "You never know." His gaze strayed toward the bedroom and he looked speculative. Poppy didn't come out. He looked back at Shane.

"Mystery woman?"

"That's right."

There was a moment of silence, then Taggart nodded. "It's what I always liked about you, Nichols. You got guts." He made a sound suspiciously like a chicken cluck.

Shane's teeth came together with a snap. His fingers balled into fists.

Taggart burst out laughing and clapped Shane on the shoulder, then turned toward the steps. "Come on. Grab your jacket. I've got a cellular phone in my saddlebag. I'll call Jed and have him meet us. We can winch your truck out, and you can leave whenever you're ready."

Shane stared after him suspiciously.

Taggart paused halfway down the steps and looked back. "Scout's honor, Nichols. I know the native curiosity of the local inhabitants. I've experienced it myself. I won't even ask."

And so it was over.

Just like that.

Taggart called Jed McCall. And while Jed drove over in his truck with the plow and the winch, Shane and

Taggart rode double on Taggart's horse to meet him at the truck.

In a matter of a little over two hours, Jed had the road from the highway plowed all the way to the cabin. Then the three of them winched Shane's truck out of the ditch and up on the snow-packed gravel.

"Thanks," Shane said to Jed while they were working the winch. He shot his brother's friend a quick, wary look, wondering if Jed would ask what he was doing here or if he'd wonder who he was with.

He needn't have worried.

"No sweat," Jed said. It was the only thing he said until they had the truck up on the road. Then, as he was getting back in his own, he looked over at Shane.

"Watch yourself," he said conversationally, with no expression on his face at all. Then he put the truck in gear and let out the clutch. As he drove off he made a noise that sounded distinctly like a chicken.

"Did you hear something?" Taggart said, grinning.

Shane's fists clenched. "No."

Taggart got back on his horse, touched a hand to the brim of his hat and gave Shane a wink. "Me, neither."

Poppy came out onto the porch as he drove up the freshly plowed road to the cabin. "That was easy," she said.

"Yeah." He got out and came toward her, wanting it not to have been so easy, wanting the snow to start up again, wanting to pretend they could keep right on with this fantasy life they'd created for themselves.

He tried looking at her, but his eyes wouldn't meet hers for longer than a second. He didn't know how to look at her now that the real world was a factor again. Everything had changed.

"Did your friend clear everything all the way to the highway?"

"He did."

"Nice of him."

He flicked a glance at her then, trying to guess if she felt the same dismay he did.

Of course she didn't, he told himself. She'd given him love, but she hadn't asked for anything back. Because she was a realist.

She'd never expect anything. Not from a guy like him.

"I better cut the fuel off," he said abruptly. "Throw the gear together, and we can go."

"I already have," Poppy said.

So she could hardly wait.

He couldn't blame her. She had a life. He was an interlude.

He wished he was a different sort of guy—a guy whom some girl might look at and think had staying power, some common sense, a future.

Any of the above.

But he wasn't.

And both of them knew it.

The ride back to town was accomplished in almost total silence. They sat side by side, but they didn't touch. For people who couldn't get enough of each other just hours before, they didn't have anything to say to each other now.

It wasn't until Shane pulled up outside her apartment and they both got out of the truck that either of them dared look at the other.

She smiled. It was a sad smile, a painful smile.

He touched her mouth with one finger. "Don't."

And then, because he was nothing if he wasn't a man of impulse, Shane indulged himself one last time.

He closed the distance between them and put his hands on her arms, drawing her into his embrace. Then, lightly, gently, he touched his lips to hers.

They were warm, soft, yielding. They parted slightly, offering him more. And he wanted more.

But he knew he had no right.

Not here. Not now. Not in the real world.

He shut his eyes and focused on the moment. He knew he would remember it even longer than he would remember their lovemaking, because it was the last time he would touch her.

He stepped back, made himself smile. Then he touched her cheek with his finger. "'Bye, Poppy Hamilton."

Then he turned and walked quickly away. He got in his truck and gunned the engine, spraying snow as he spun away from the curb. He stared straight ahead.

He wasn't looking back, not for anything in the world.

Eight

He was gone.

One minute he was there, holding her, and the next...he wasn't.

He was gone.

One minute he was there, kissing her, making her wish and hope and dream of forever.

And the next...he wasn't.

Of course he wasn't, Poppy told herself firmly. She'd never expected he would be.

But oh, God, how she'd wished!

And still he'd gone.

Poppy stood quite still, watching—even then, hoping—until his truck had rumbled down the street and around the corner.

He was gone.

She was alone. And then, only then, had she turned and trudged up the stairs—back to real life.

Her cat was mad. Her plants were thirsty. Newspapers were piling up outside her door. Her answering machine was flashing more times than she wanted to count.

Poppy apologized to the cat and refilled his not-quite-empty food dish. She watered her plants and apologized to them, too. She carried in her newspapers and dumped them straight into the trash. She shut off the answering machine without listening to a word. The phone started ringing even as she did so. She ignored it.

She was back in the real world, all right, the world she had coped with day after day for twenty-five years without thinking about it.

She thought about it now.

She wanted to be back in the cabin with Shane.

Get over it, she told herself sharply. *You knew it wouldn't last.*

And, of course, that was only the truth.

But knowing something and facing the reality of it were two different things as she had pointed out just the day before when she had told Shane about her mother's death.

She had known her mother was dying. She had known that their days in the cabin would end. In both cases she had faced reality head-on—and been ground into the dirt in the process, she thought wryly.

Do you learn from your experience? she asked herself.

No.

Not very bright, are you?

No, not very.

The phone stopped ringing. She kicked off her shoes and fell onto her bed. It should have felt soft, comfortable, familiar. It felt foreign.

Comfortable and familiar would have been to fall into the bed at the cabin and into Shane Nichols's arms.

"You are a nut case," Poppy said out loud.

No, she corrected herself. She was stressed.

She'd been kidnapped, hadn't she?

She'd been taken away against her will, held in a mountain cabin for three days, kissed within an inch of her life, loved until she couldn't see straight, and then brought back to face a furious cat and what was doubtless a tape full of cranky messages from her father.

"It would make anyone insane," she assured herself as she rolled over onto her back and hauled a pillow against her breasts and hugged it hard. "Anyone," she repeated, as if saying it again would convince her.

Maybe it did, for in her mind now she didn't see her room anymore. As she shut her eyes, she saw the cabin, all rough logs and plank floors. And she didn't feel the pillow anymore. She felt Shane's weight atop her and his arms around her. It wasn't the cool percale of the pillowcase against her cheek, either, but the moist roughness of Shane's three-day-old beard.

Moist roughness?

Poppy's eyes flew open.

The cat blinked right in her face, made a small disapproving sound, then went back to licking her cheek.

"Ergh," Poppy muttered and rolled away from him. "Go away, Wally."

But Wally didn't go away. He stepped onto her back and began kneading. And there was nothing about his little cat paws that reminded her of Shane. She didn't have a man. She had a cat.

Oh, yes, she was back.

This was her life.

"So get on with it," she muttered to herself.

She would. Tomorrow.

Tomorrow she would call her father, read her mail, open her shop, do her job, meet an eligible man.

Tonight she would sleep.

And maybe, with luck, she would dream about Shane.

"What do you mean, how was the wedding? You weren't there?" Amber, the girl who was helping in Poppy's Garden while Milly was on her honeymoon, looked astonished at Poppy's question.

Poppy had been in the shop since six. She hadn't slept well. She hadn't dreamed of Shane—only of messages from her father—and she'd had nothing to stay in bed for.

Obviously God was trying to point out that she'd shirked long enough.

So she got up and made a pot of black coffee and ate some dry toast, and told herself that she was feeling much better, thank you. It was a necessary lie, she assured herself. If she kept repeating it, eventually it would be true.

In the meantime, she would carry on as if those days at the cabin with Shane hadn't even happened.

And now she wondered if they hadn't!

How on earth could Amber not even notice that she hadn't shown up at Milly and Mike's wedding?

"I...had to go out of town," she said vaguely, plucking some mums out of a vase. "A spur-of-the-moment thing. I'm sorry to have missed it. It must have been wonderful."

Amber shrugged out of her coat and hung it up. "Wonderful? Hardly. But it was pretty interesting. Cash barging in that way, striding down the aisle in the middle of the ceremony like he was in some movie!"

Poppy stopped pushing mums into a foam block and gaped. "Cash did *what?*"

"Stopped the wedding," Amber said cheerfully. "Didn't you know? Where were you? The North Pole?"

"Something like that." Poppy's mind reeled. "Out of town. I told you. Tell me what happened?"

"Well, the wedding was going along just fine. Real pretty. Except Milly was a little ticked 'cause you left those flowers for her to do in the morning."

Poppy let that pass. "Go on."

"It didn't really matter in the end 'cause no one will ever remember that."

"What happened?"

"The minister was just starting to do the marriage thing, when all of a sudden there was this commotion in the back, and one of the ushers said, 'Hey, you can't go in there!' and Cash said, 'Like to see you try an' stop me!' An' the usher did, an' next thing you know, the usher was lying on the floor and Cash was comin' up the aisle!"

"Cash *hit* one of Mike's ushers?"

"Well, the story is supposed to be that the usher slipped on some melting ice," Amber said piously, but the grin came creeping back. "But he's got a black eye today."

"Oh, dear God." Poppy strangled the mum.

"Cash stepped over him, went down to the front, looked Milly straight in the eye and told her he'd step back and never say another word if she'd swear to him in front of all these people that she didn't love him anymore." Amber paused dramatically.

"And?" Poppy prompted. "And?"

"And she couldn't! She started cryin', and her mother started cryin' and her father said, 'Oh, for God's sake!'

and Mike didn't say anything, and the preacher didn't, either. I don't think he knew what to say.''

"They probably don't get lessons in that sort of thing at the seminary,'' Poppy said. Her mind was reeling.

Cash had done that? Cash had come back, punched somebody out and broken up the wedding of the woman he loved?

What would he have done if he'd come back to discover that there wasn't a wedding because the night before, his buddy had run off with the bride?

"Oh, Lord,'' she muttered.

Amber rolled her eyes. "Pretty wild, huh?''

"You have no idea,'' Poppy said faintly. What would Shane say when he heard?

"Milly just kept crying. And then she started apologizing to Mike, and Mike looked as if he'd like to punch Cash.''

"He didn't?'' Poppy said hopefully.

"No. He just looked disgusted. Then he said to Milly, 'You want him? Fine. You got 'im. I'd rather know now.' And he walked out. Nobody else moved. They all waited, looking at Milly and Cash. Then Cash said there was no reason to waste the wedding. All it needed was a new groom. And that would suit him just fine. Milly said, 'Well, it doesn't suit me!' and slapped him! Too bad you missed it.''

"Indeed,'' Poppy murmured. "And where are Cash and Milly now?''

"Who knows? She went storming out, still crying. And Cash just sort of shrugged and said he was sorry if he'd ruined everybody's party, but if they wanted to go to The Barrel, drinks were on him. I think he wanted to give Milly a little time to cool off.''

"Smart of him,'' Poppy said.

Amber nodded. "So where'd you go?"

"Er, just...away for the weekend with a...friend."

"In all that snow?"

"It wasn't snowing that badly when I left," Poppy lied.

"It was snowing like crazy. He must've been pretty special," Amber said slyly.

"What makes you think it was a he?"

"Had to be. You wouldn't have done anything that dumb otherwise."

"It wasn't dumb."

"Not if he was the right guy," Amber agreed.

Right before closing her father came in.

"You knew, didn't you?" he said without preamble.

Poppy, who was putting the finishing touches on an anniversary bouquet and thinking for the hundredth time that day about Shane's lovemaking, started guiltily and stared at him. "Knew? Knew what?"

"That Callahan was going to come barging in there and make an ass out of himself! True love conquering all." The Honorable Judge George Winthrop Hamilton gave an ungentlemanly snort and stalked around the shop, nearly knocking over a hothouse palm.

"Well, it was sort of romantic," Poppy ventured. Hadn't *he* noticed she wasn't there, either?

"Told you he was going to do it, did he?"

"What? No, of course not."

He stopped, turned and leveled a stare in her direction. "Then how'd you know not to be there?"

So he had noticed. "I...er, had an errand to run."

"Long errand," he said shortly. "You were gone three days."

"An out-of-town errand," Poppy said hastily.

His gaze got narrower. "You were supposed to be at the wedding. You were doing flowers for the wedding. That's what you told me, anyway. And I said I'd bring young Phillips to meet you. Or is that why you weren't there?"

Poppy shook her head. "No. I'd just had a pressing commitment. I'd...love to meet him sometime," she said vaguely. "I'm sure he's...very nice."

"Nice." Her father fairly spat the word. "Nice never cut ice! Phillips is strong, tough. Right out of the old school. Plus he's got a good brain. He's going to be one of Montana's most powerful men one day. You watch."

"I will." She just didn't intend to do it from across the breakfast table.

Her father scowled and did another lap around her shop. "Didn't matter that you weren't there," he said finally. "Phillips couldn't be there, either. He had an appointment in Helena. At least he called." He fixed Poppy with a glare that told her she hadn't been forgiven her lapse in manners.

Her father didn't sound all that pleased with his perfect Mr. Phillips, though, either. He rarely had to deal with someone too busy to be at his beck and call. And he made a harrumphing sound that told Poppy he was displeased at having to admit it.

"Said he'd come in the next week or two. I'll call you when he's going to be here," he went on. "Then you can come out to the house to meet him. No excuses this time. Cook him a good meal. Your mother's stuffed roast recipe."

"Dad, I don't—"

He placed his palms flat on the counter and leaned toward her. "He's a good catch, Poppy. Good man. Good education. Good job. Family owns half a county.

He'll make some woman a good husband. And time will come when he'll need a good wife.'' He looked at her pointedly.

"He might want to pick his own," Poppy suggested mildly.

"No time," her father said. "Busy man. Figured I'd help him out a little."

Poppy groaned. "Dad, that's not how it's done these days."

"It's how I do it," Judge Hamilton told his only daughter. He plucked a drooping daisy off at the stem and tossed it in the trash. "I'll call you when I get a date set up."

"Thought we'd lost you."

"What?" Shane blinked. He'd been staring out the window, seeing not the kids playing in the snow, but Poppy loving him. He hadn't heard a word that Jenny had said.

So what else was new? He hadn't heard much of anything since he'd got back to the ranch three days before.

"I said, I thought when you didn't come back last weekend that you'd decided you'd rehabbed enough. I thought you'd gone and done something stupid—like entered a rodeo."

"No," Shane said.

He'd done something stupid, all right, just not that.

"I'm glad," Jenny said. She smiled at him.

He managed a wan smile in return, then went back to staring out the window, still not watching the kids, just trying to relive those days with Poppy. And not just the hours when they'd made love. No, he wanted it all—the meals, the smiles, the teasing, the talking, the snowballs and the silliness, the serious conversation and the quiet sighs.

He'd wanted it ever since he'd driven off and left her. He'd told himself he would forget about her. He was a master at forgetting, at turning his back and moving on. He couldn't begin to remember the names of the women he'd been with over the years.

He couldn't imagine ever forgetting Poppy.

"—all right?"

He was suddenly aware that Jenny was still standing there. "Huh?"

"I asked if you were all right? Ever since you came back you've been—I don't know—different. Quieter." She crossed the room and put her palm against his forehead. "No fever," she said.

"I'm not sick!"

"Well, you're not normal, either."

He couldn't dispute that. He shrugged irritably. "I'm getting antsy," he said. "Too much time in one place. It does that to a guy. I oughta be gettin' on down the road."

"A month the doctor said. At a minimum. You need more time to heal."

"My hand might. I don't."

That was what was wrong with him—not Poppy Hamilton. The reason he was obsessing about her was that he didn't have anything better to do. "Reckon it's time for me to be on my way."

"Where would you go?"

"Don't matter," Shane said stubbornly. "I got friends. Reckon I'll just head out. See what I can see."

"That's crazy," Jenny said.

The door opened and her husband came in, a son

clinging to each arm, a daughter hanging around his neck.

"Mace, Shane's talking about leaving!"

Shane nodded firmly. "You know I'm not cut out for this settled routine."

Mace looked skeptical. "A man can change."

"Not me."

"You're gonna have to one of these days," Mace said mildly.

But Shane shook his head. "Not yet."

He wasn't ready to call it quits yet. He'd been to the edge of the abyss, but he still couldn't look over. There would be time to do that. He had his whole damn life to do that! But not now. Not yet.

Slowly Mace shrugged. "Suit yourself."

"But—" Jenny began.

"It's not up to us," Mace said to his wife, looking briefly at her, but then letting his gaze swing back to meet his brother's. "It's your call," he said.

"That's right. It's my call. I'll be on my way at first light."

It was just what he needed: a wide-open road, a new vista, the horizon spread out before him.

He felt the surge of adrenaline the minute he drove away from Mace and Jenny's ranch.

It wasn't that he didn't love them. He did. He loved the kids, too. They added something he hadn't even realized was missing in his brother's life until the three of them were there. Now he couldn't imagine Mace and Jenny without them.

"Why are you goin'?" Pilar had demanded. His niece had hung on his arm almost from the moment she'd learned Uncle Shane was going away.

"Got to," he'd said, throwing his clothes into his duffel and setting his rigging bag by the door.

"Why? Is somebody makin' you?" she'd asked. She had started first grade this past fall. She understood now how other people could make you do things.

But Shane shook his head. "Nobody's making me."

Pilar drew her knees up against her chest and wrapped her skinny arms around them. "Then why are you goin'? Don't you love us anymore?"

Shane looked up. "Of course I love you."

"Then are you leavin' 'cause it's for our own good?"

He tried to figure out what she was thinking. Probably it had to do with her South American grandmother who couldn't take care of her and her brothers anymore and had sent them to Mace and Jenny. Pilar knew it wasn't because their grandmother hadn't loved them. She had done it "for their own good."

But Shane couldn't even say that. He shrugged.

"Maybe he's runnin' away," his nephew Mark suggested.

Shane's eyes had flashed. "I am *not* running away."

He wasn't, he assured himself now, as he headed down the road away from home and family. And Poppy.

Of course he wasn't.

She would forget. It would just take time.

And a good thing, too, because time was something Poppy had an abundance of.

She had her work, and her cat and phone calls from her father about his progress in lining up the elusive J.R. Phillips.

But J.R. Phillips was so busy that he was becoming a distant threat as the days passed. Poppy's life settled into a routine again.

At first she thought maybe Shane would drop by. She knew he'd been staying with his brother and sister-in-law on their ranch northwest of Elmer. That wasn't so far, she assured herself. He could drive down to Livingston in little more than half an hour.

But he didn't come.

Then she told herself it was just as well. If she saw him, what would she say? Worse, what would she do?

Would she be able to pretend indifference?

God knew she hadn't mastered indifference on the inside. Perhaps she was lucky he wasn't testing her ability to display it for public consumption.

Still, it didn't stop her from glancing up hopefully every time the door opened, even after a week went by.

But always it was customers.

Until the following Monday when the door opened and Milly walked in.

Poppy wasn't exactly surprised. It was the day Milly was supposed to have come back to work after her honeymoon with Mike. But even though there had obviously been no honeymoon, she hadn't appeared last week. Poppy hadn't wanted to call her.

Now she thumped her backpack down on the counter and shed her jacket without speaking.

Poppy looked up from the cyclamens she was watering and gave Milly a wary smile. "Hi."

Milly grunted.

"If you don't feel like working, you can go home," Poppy offered a little hesitantly.

Milly looked up, eyes flashing. "Why wouldn't I feel like working? What else would I be doing if I weren't here?"

"I don't know," Poppy said, at a loss. "What have you been doing?"

"You mean, since I didn't get married?"

Poppy nodded awkwardly. "I should have called you. I didn't know what to say." And not just about Cash, either.

"Who does?" Milly said bitterly. "How dare he? How dare he think he can just bust into my wedding and destroy my life!"

"Did he?" Poppy asked. "Destroy your life?"

Milly gave her a sharp look.

"Well, I mean, if you don't love Mike...and you do love Cash..."

"Did you *know*? Did he *tell* you?" she demanded. She set to work repotting some begonias and Poppy feared silently for their lives.

"Of course he didn't tell me! I didn't see him before he—"

"You didn't see him there, either," Milly accused. She picked up a potting knife and began cutting apart a flat of begonia seedlings. "You didn't come. You left the flowers for me to finish! Where were you?"

Poppy concentrated on the cyclamens. "I...got tied up. It was...unavoidable." She didn't think, under the circumstances, she wanted to add to the stories that would forever surround Milly's nonwedding.

"A man," Milly translated bitterly. She slapped her hand on the counter. "To hell with men."

"They're not all terrible," Poppy said. "Cash obviously loves you."

"Cash is crazy! He thinks that he can just show up, ruin my wedding, chase off my fiancé, and I'll fall into his arms like a ripe plum."

"I take it you won't?"

"I told him to go to hell." Sniffling, Milly stabbed a begonia. Then the sniffles turned to sobs, and she dropped the potting knife and groped in her pocket for a tissue. "Damn," she mumbled. "Oh, damn."

"Milly," Poppy said gently, "go home."

Milly rubbed her eyes. "No." Her tone was defiant. So was the look she gave Poppy. "I don't want to go home. Home is worse than anywhere. My mother thinks I should talk to him. My father thinks he should shoot him. I've listened to both of them for over a week! I need to get out, to work, to be here."

Poppy gave her a wry look. "You won't be much good selling flowers with red eyes and a blotchy face."

"I'll tell them I'm allergic."

"And that will help sales enormously, I'm sure," Poppy said dryly.

Milly gave one last sniffle. "All right, I won't. But don't send me home, Poppy. Please. I need to keep busy." She gulped and picked up the potting knife again. "I just need to stop thinking about it. About *him*," she admitted. "I hate him. And I love him. Nothing makes sense."

Poppy could relate to that.

Shane closed bars with his buddies all the way from Elmer to Spokane. Then he headed south, looking for warmer weather.

"'Reckon I'll find myself a gal in a bikini and take it easy for a while," he told his pal Martin in Oregon on his way through.

And when he stopped in Red Bluff, his old traveling partner's sister, Dori, had a red bikini. But somehow Shane couldn't dredge up the appetite for taking it easy with her. Besides it was raining in Red Bluff. It wasn't close enough to the ocean. He kept moving on.

He stopped in Santa Maria to see another friend. It

was closer to the ocean. It wasn't raining. But Norm didn't have any sisters, and his wife's sisters weren't, she told him firmly, about to be corrupted by him.

"What makes you think I'd corrupt 'em?" Shane asked.

"I know you," Betty Lou answered.

Did she?

Shane didn't think he even knew himself anymore.

Certainly nothing that used to appeal to him seemed appealing any longer. The call of the open road didn't beckon the way it used to. The notion that there were brighter lights and prettier women over the next hill held no enticement.

He told himself it was because he wasn't competing. The purpose had gone out of his life.

That was, of course, the truth. But he didn't dwell on it. He dwelt on Poppy.

And then he shoved her out of his mind.

She would be out for good when he got back to competing, when his life returned to normal. Soon. Please God, real soon.

He'd checked with the doctor in Portland when he passed through. Doc Reeves thought the thumb looked pretty good. He took the cast and bandages off. He manipulated it slowly.

"Bend it like this," he said, demonstrating with his own.

Shane tried to. It felt stiff and awkward, like he was trying to move somebody else's thumb. "I'll get better," he assured the doctor quickly. "I'll work at it. Be back to those bulls in no time." He grinned.

The doctor had nodded and glanced down at Shane's medical records. "You're thirty-two now?"

Thirty-two wasn't old, damn it! It was the prime of a man's life! The height of his powers. His best years.

Unless he made his living riding bulls, Shane thought grimly now.

He would find something else, he remembered Poppy telling him.

What? he wanted to ask her.

He wanted to share his misery with her. He wanted to kiss her and touch her and make love over and over to her.

But Poppy was in Montana. And he was...

Hell, he couldn't even remember where he was anymore.

Nine

Poppy and Milly went out on a double date.

It was perhaps not the brightest thing either of them had ever done. But desperation made fools of lots of women.

"They're nice men," Poppy had assured Milly. "Kyle is everything I could want in a man. He's dependable and kind and respectful and—"

"He sounds like a lapdog," Milly grumbled.

Poppy had been inclined to think the same thing whenever she'd run into high school journalism teacher, Kyle Raymond. But she had to do something to distract herself.

So when she saw him at the grocery store, and he suggested going to Bozeman to a movie on a night when she'd promised Milly to join her in watching reruns of "Welcome Back, Kotter," well, admitting the truth only encouraged him.

"Milly can come, too," he said brightly. "With Larry."

Larry Pitts was the high school football coach. Like Kyle he was single and lonely.

"I don't know," Poppy hedged. But eventually she allowed herself to be convinced. She even convinced Milly.

"You need to get on with your life," she told Milly. "If you're not going to marry Mike and you're not going to marry Cash, why not go out with someone else?"

"What if he wants to marry me?" Milly had asked with gallows humor.

But in the end, she went.

It was not a memorable evening. Kyle was everything Poppy had said he was. Larry was better than Milly had had any right to hope.

But Kyle wasn't Shane, and Larry wasn't Cash.

Milly said, "I can't do this," and declined Larry's suggestion of a second date.

Poppy was made of sterner stuff.

When Kyle called and asked her to drive to Billings with him the following Saturday night for a concert, she said, "That sounds like fun," in such a bright voice that Milly, who was snipping baby's breath and shamelessly eavesdropping, groaned and rolled her eyes.

"You don't love him," she said when Poppy hung up.

"I don't have to love him to go to a concert with him."

"You're never going to love him," Milly went on relentlessly.

"I'm never going to know that unless I go out with him, am I?" Poppy said logically.

"You know. Love hits you between the eyes like a

hammer,'' Milly said glumly. ''You're never the same again.''

''I don't think I believe that,'' Poppy said.

But she was beginning to.

It had been three weeks since Shane had kidnapped her, loved her and left her.

And she was no nearer forgetting him than she was to falling in love with Kyle.

''Good news.''

The voice on the other end of the line rocked Poppy out of a restless sleep. ''Good morning, Daddy,'' she mumbled, prying open her eyes and seeing that it was just after 6:00 a.m on the Sunday morning after the Billings concert.

Only her father could find good news this early on a weekend morning.

''What news?'' she asked, burrowing back under the covers, wishing for sleep, wishing for the dream he'd rocked her awake from—a dream in which she was back at the cabin with Shane.

''J.R. will be here Friday night. I've invited him for dinner.''

Poppy groaned.

''Don't be obstinate. He's everything you could want in a man, Poppy,'' her father said sternly. ''Everything.'' He didn't say, *Everything Chad wasn't*. But his firmness underlined his conviction. ''He's clever. He's bright. He's honest. He has scruples. Besides that he's well-off. Handsome. He doesn't mind a working wife. He—''

''You *asked* him?'' Poppy squeaked, sitting bolt upright.

''Of course I asked him,'' her father said stiffly. ''I don't want to propose someone unsuitable.''

Of course not, Poppy thought woefully.

"Trust me, Poppy. I have your best interests at heart. And you know you've always wanted a husband and family. Ever since you were a little girl you said you wanted lots of children."

"Yes, but—"

"And you can't have them without a husband."

"Well, I could," Poppy began.

But he cut her off firmly. "You won't."

"No, I won't. But—"

"And I've always wanted to be a grandfather," he went on, a new, wistful quality in his voice now.

Poppy felt small and guilty.

"J.R. will make a wonderful father. Like I said, dear, he's perfect for you."

He might very well be perfect, Poppy thought.

But he wasn't Shane.

"So take a date," Milly said between bites of a peanut butter sandwich. She was not precisely sympathetic when Poppy gave her the grim news on Monday morning. "You can take Cash if you want," she offered.

"You're speaking to him?"

"No. But my mother is. I could get my mother to ask him."

But Poppy shook her head. "No. It wouldn't be convincing. And after what Cash did, my father would make mincemeat out of him."

"Not a bad idea," Milly said darkly. She chewed her sandwich thoughtfully. "What about Kyle?"

"No." Kyle was too nice. More mincemeat.

"Larry is pretty tough," Milly offered after a moment.

"I don't think so."

Even Larry wouldn't be a match for her father and the perfect man because Poppy knew she wouldn't be able to muster up any enthusiasm toward him. Her father would interpret her bringing Larry for exactly what it was—a desperate attempt to ward off the inevitable.

There was only one man she knew who could make her father stop and pause for thought—only one man she could take who could convince her father that he was far more interesting than any "perfect husband material" the judge provided.

One man.

She didn't dare.

They hadn't seen each other in weeks. Surely if he'd been interested, he would have called or come by.

And yet she couldn't help remembering that what had happened between them had not been one-sided.

He's probably like that with all women, she told herself sharply.

But somehow she didn't think so. Shane might be a "hail fellow well met" in general, but she didn't think he let many people inside.

She actually suspected that the surface charm was less the whole of his personality than a defense to keep people from knowing the real Shane.

"And when did you get a degree in psychology?" she jibed aloud.

Milly blinked. "What?"

"Nothing," Poppy mumbled. "Just thinking."

"Think fast," Milly advised. "Friday isn't far away."

He wanted to call home.

He wanted to talk to Mace and Jenny. He wanted to hear more about Mark's new horse and Tony's snow fort. He wanted Jenny to hold the phone next to the piano so Pilar could play her newest piece for him.

He especially wanted to ask if they'd been to Livingston lately, if by chance they'd happened into that little florist's shop called Poppy's Garden, if they'd seen the dark-haired woman who owned it, if she was every bit as beautiful as he remembered, if she looked as sleepless and washed out as he did. If she, too, felt like hell.

He didn't let himself call.

He wasn't some homesick kid. He hadn't been hanging around telephone booths even when he was eighteen. He had hit the road and never looked back.

Oh, he'd called now and then. But he hadn't thought about it constantly. On the contrary, he'd almost never thought about home. It was just the way he was, he told himself. For Shane Nichols, out of sight had been out of mind.

"Yeah," he muttered to himself as he tried to avoid even looking at the phone on the wall of the grocery store in Prescott. "Well, look at you now."

He had, after all, called just last week.

He'd talked to Mace and Jenny then. He'd heard about the horse and the snow fort, and Pilar had played him a song about somebody she called Claire Doubloon.

But he hadn't asked about the florist shop down in Livingston. He didn't know anything new about Poppy.

And he wouldn't if he called now.

Because he'd never mentioned her to any of them. Had never let her name drop from his lips. Had brushed off Jenny's questions about those days he'd been stranded in the cabin. Had ignored Mace's speculative looks.

If no one knew, he could pretend she didn't matter.

But she did.

He could pretend he would forget her. He damned well would if he could.

He bought his groceries. He stowed them in the truck. Then he went back in and called home, anyway.

Just to say hi. Just to touch base. To hear the voices of some people who'd be glad to hear from him.

"How are you?" he asked when Jenny answered.

"Fine." She sounded surprised, but not displeased, to hear from him. "How are you?"

"I'm doin' good," he said. He flexed his thumb. "Real good." Did his voice sound as hollow to her ears as it did to his?

"I'm glad. Where are you?"

"Prescott. Arizona."

"Oh. That's a long way," she said doubtfully. "Too long," she added after a moment's pause.

"Too long for what?"

"To come for dinner."

"Dinner? You want me to come to dinner?"

"Not me. Someone called Poppy."

"Poppy? Er, this is—"

"Shane!" At least she sounded glad to hear from him. So that probably meant she wasn't inviting him to dinner to serve him with an arrest warrant. She wasn't going to lure him in and have her dad lying in wait with a cop to slap the handcuffs on him.

Actually he never thought she would. It was just an excuse to keep from calling her.

He'd done probably thirty laps around the supermarket parking lot after he'd hung up from talking to Jenny, trying to decide what to do.

"I told her you were miles away by now," Jenny had

said. "But that I'd tell you if you called. I told her not to get her hopes up."

So he hadn't had to call. He could have pretended he never got the message, or didn't get it in time. It would have been smarter. Saner.

But he was Shane Nichols. When had *sane* and *smart* ever mattered when he was making up his mind what to do?

He called.

"Yeah, uh, hi." He cleared his throat which felt suddenly dry. "Jenny...um...my sister-in-law...said you called and—" Cripes, he was sweating just talking to her.

No. He was sweating because this was Arizona and it was hot. Well, it wasn't actually *that* hot, but—

"She said she didn't know where you were. You're home?" Poppy said hopefully.

"Not exactly." He was comforted by the fact that Poppy sounded a little hesitant, too. But wonderful. Shane could envision her, that wary expression on her face, that look of hope in her hazel eyes. He propped himself up against the wall of the supermarket and tucked the phone against his shoulder.

"I just called her. She gave me your message. Dinner, she said?" He tried to make the word casual, but it came out eager.

"Well, yes. I was...hoping...that you could come. But she said—"

"Friday?" Jenny'd told him Friday.

"I know it's short notice but—"

To a guy who'd never asked a girl for a date more than half an hour ahead of time, it seemed like a million years. And so he was in Arizona? So what? He'd driven more hours and more miles to get to a rodeo, where chances were he would get kicked in the head.

"I'll be there."

"Wonderful!" She sounded overjoyed. "Six o'clock. At my father's."

"*What?*" He almost dropped the phone. He stood bolt upright and gripped the receiver in a stranglehold.

"I'm sorry. I forgot to tell you. It's at my father's place. It's...because he's come up with his perfect man. Remember? I told you he was going to try to do that. And now he has."

She sounded desperate.

Shane felt desperate. "You want me to eat dinner with you and your father and...his idea of a perfect man?" No wonder he was sweating.

"You don't have to *do* anything," Poppy said. "Just...just *be* there. He expects me to show up and cook the meal, smile and say all the right things. Be perfect wife material. And I can't!" This last was a wail.

"Oh, God."

There was a long silence on the other end of the line, but she didn't offer to let him off the hook. "I know you had a run-in with him," she said quietly. "But you were a kid then, weren't you? I mean, it was a long time ago?"

"Not long enough," Shane muttered.

"He won't remember."

"He'll remember."

"He won't care."

"He'll care."

"Shane!" she said, exasperated. "Please."

"Poppy... No." His mouth went totally dry just thinking about it. The man had made him a laughing-stock. And as far as driving off any eligible suitors went...

There was a dollar's worth of long distance silence. Then Poppy said, "You owe me."

"What?"

"You heard me. You owe me this. I kept my mouth shut about my 'kidnapping.' I—"

"Commandeering," Shane corrected sharply.

"Kidnapping," she repeated firmly. "I never told anyone. And believe me I could have! Everyone and the cat wanted to know where I was that weekend and who I was with! They all think I'm some sort of woman of mystery now who sneaks off with equally mysterious men."

"So what's wrong with that?"

"I'm *not* mysterious! I'm a liar. I said I wouldn't be. But I am. And if I've got to be a liar for you, the least you can do is be one for me. Just show up for dinner. And pretend you're interested in me."

I *am* interested in you, he wanted to yell at her.

"Why me?" he demanded.

"Because you're the only one who...who— Just trust me. You're the only one he'd believe."

"He'd get out his gun."

Poppy sighed. "I need you, Shane. I thought you...I thought we—" She stopped. The silence went on. And on. Then, "Never mind," she said dully. "It doesn't matter."

But it did.

Shane knew it did. He knew the moment he got over his knee-jerk reaction to having to see her father again, that it mattered a lot.

He didn't just want to help her out, pretending to *be* the man in her life. He wanted to *be* the man in her life.

"I'll be there."

* * *

The next day Poppy called Shane's brother's house again.

"I gave him your message," his sister-in-law told her. "But he was in Arizona, and—"

"Arizona!" She hadn't realized. She'd called to leave a message that he didn't have to come, that she'd thought better of it, that she had no right to coerce him. She wanted him to—desperately—but not because she'd forced him to.

Now she was sure, despite his quiet "I'll be there" that he wouldn't.

"He called me yesterday afternoon," she told Jenny. "And I thought he said he'd be able to come. I was going to tell him he didn't have to. But if he's in Arizona...well, I must have misunderstood."

"I don't think so," Jenny said. "If he said he'd come, he will. Shane never promises anything unless he plans to deliver."

"But—"

"You don't want him?"

"I—" But she couldn't say she didn't want him. "Will you just tell him if he calls?"

"I'll tell him," Jenny promised.

And probably she had.

But on Friday, standing in her father's kitchen cooking dinner, Poppy prayed he hadn't got the message. She wanted Shane to be there.

Still, she didn't expect him. If he actually did drive all the way back to Montana, surely he would go to the ranch first. His sister-in-law would give him the message, and that would be that. He might be angry that he'd driven all this way for nothing. But mostly she thought he would be relieved that she'd changed her mind and didn't expect him to come.

It was the best she could do.

She tried not to think about him as she put her mother's good damask tablecloth on the table and got out her parents' wedding silver and the bone china that her father had given her mother on their tenth anniversary.

She'd decided not to make her mother's wonderful garlic-stuffed roast. She never did it as well as her mother had.

So she went for the tried-and-true—a standard all-American turkey dinner with all the trimmings. It was subtle perhaps, but if he was as bright as her father claimed, maybe he would see the signs. Maybe the turkey and dressing, mashed potatoes and gravy, cranberry sauce and green bean casserole would be so tradition-bound, would shout so loudly of home and hearth that they would drive J.R. Phillips away.

She couldn't imagine any man of a marriageable age not running in the other direction if an unattached woman cooked it for him. Unless he truly was looking for a wife.

She still had hopes that, regardless of what her father said, J.R. Phillips was as marriage shy as she was.

And if he wasn't, well, she would get rid of him somehow. Politely, of course.

But it would have been easier if she'd been able to flaunt Shane.

And there she was, thinking about him again. Damn it.

She glanced out the window and saw the flash of sun on the windshield of a vehicle coming up the lane. Her father, no doubt, with the perfect man in tow.

She wiped damp palms on the sides of her apron, then headed back to the kitchen.

She busied herself there with last-minute preparations, not wanting to be caught hovering by the door, but listening for it to open and her father's voice to ring out.

She heard the doorbell instead.

Drat. She hadn't counted on him sending J.R. on ahead.

But, she thought hopefully as she shed her apron and hung it on a hook by the door, maybe it was for the best. This way she could set J.R. Phillips straight before her father even got here.

Pasting on her best-polite hostess smile, she opened the door.

It was Shane.

Jenny had told him he didn't have to go.

"Your Poppy called," she'd told him when he drove into the yard last night. "She said to tell you that you don't have to come." She was giving him curious, assessing looks, and he knew she was wondering who this Poppy was.

He ignored the looks and went to the message, which had rocked him. "You're saying she doesn't want me?"

"I'm not exactly saying that," Jenny said.

"What *are* you saying?" Shane demanded, exasperated.

"Just what she told me. That you didn't have to come."

"I didn't drive all this way to turn around now," he said flatly.

Jenny's brows lifted. Her eyes widened. "She must be pretty special," Jenny murmured.

Shane met his sister-in-law's gaze steadily. "She is."

And so he was here.

Early. And determined.

And when she opened the door, he felt such a rush of joy at the sight of her that he wondered why in God's name he'd stayed away so long.

"So," he drawled, smiling, "am I still invited. Or not?"

She blinked the same way Jenny had at seeing him. Then a smile dawned on her face that was even better than the ones he'd spent a month dreaming about.

She launched herself into his arms. "Oh, yes. Oh, Shane. Yes!"

And as he caught her, all the aching need and desperate desire that had been building within him for the past month took over. He wrapped his arms around her and pressed his lips to hers.

It was like coming home.

It was warmth and welcome and just a hint of the wildness he had known when he was loving her. It awakened all the urgency he'd told himself all month he didn't feel. It stirred cravings he'd tried to convince himself he didn't have.

"Poppy!" His fingers loosed the pins that bound her hair, tangling in the silken strands, all the time his mouth was fused with hers. Their bodies, too, could not seem to get close enough. He felt her hands slide up under his jacket, then tug at his shirttails. He shifted to make it easier for her to free them from his jeans and was rewarded seconds later by the feel of her hands on his bare back.

With one hand still tangling in her hair, he let the other tease the waistband of her skirt, then burrow inside to stroke her heated skin.

"I missed you," he mumbled against her mouth. "Oh, God, I missed you! The whole time I was out there, I might as well have been going in circles, because in my head I was with you.''

"Yes," Poppy said. "Yes! Oh, me, too.''

Then they were kissing again, hungrily, greedily, desperately.

The door opened. A rush of cold February air slammed in.

"Are we interrupting something?" asked Poppy's father.

Ten

It was not a *Miss Manners* moment.

Or if it was, Poppy had skipped that chapter, certain it would never happen to her.

"Oh, God," she muttered under her breath. With one frantic, trembling hand she groped to tuck in her blouse, while the other attempted to do something constructive to her undone hair.

She glanced at Shane. His normally tanned face was white. He was stuffing his shirt back into his jeans. Had she pulled it out? Poppy realized with mounting embarrassment that she had.

"D-Daddy," she said with as much brightness as she could muster. "You're...early?"

Her father looked pointedly at his watch. "Right on time."

"Ah." Poppy finished the desperate jamming of her

blouse and raked her fingers through her hair. "Of course. Time…must have got away from me."

"No doubt," her father said stonily.

But he barely glanced at her.

His gaze was focused entirely on Shane, and he was looking just short of murderous. His normally pale complexion was florid. His fingers were balled into fists.

And Shane didn't look much better. Rather like an animal trapped in a hunter's sights—desperate, determined. And wild.

Poppy wondered if they would battle it out right here.

"Shane?" An unexpected unknown voice broke in. *"Nichols?* What the hell are you doing here?"

Shane jerked. He looked past her father at the man who'd come in behind him. A man who was looking at Shane, not with murderous intent, but surprise and— pleasure?

Shane's eyes widened. He looked, if possible, even more stricken. *"Rance?"*

"Hey, buddy, George didn't tell me you'd be here." The man came forward to pump Shane's hand eagerly. "But then," he added with a grin and a wink, "I guess maybe he didn't know."

Color burned now in Shane's cheeks. He gave himself a little shake, like a dog shedding water. Poppy saw him swallow, then steady himself. A mask seemed to come over his face. He looked composed now, expressionless, except for the wry smile that fleetingly touched his mouth.

"Rance," he said again, gripping the other man's hand. There was something new in his voice now—a sort of quiet resignation. "I might have known it would be you."

* * *

Judge Hamilton, his nemesis. Rance Phillips, his savior.

Shane supposed there was a certain ironic symmetry to this. He supposed maybe God was trying to tell him something.

He was afraid he knew what....

It had begun fourteen years ago during his senior year of high school on the day before the football game between the Murray High Hawks and the Elmer Eagles.

The trans-mountain rivalry between the schools had always been intense, having gone back to an actual gunfight between an Elmer ne'er-do-well and a Murray scapegrace eighty-odd years before.

Each side had blamed the other. And when it wasn't acceptable to go gunning for each other anymore, the animosity had found its outlet in football.

Murray had won the last three years running. Shane thought the streak had gone on far too long. The way to turn the tide, he told his friend Jake, was to use psychology.

"Take away their pride," he had said.

"What pride?" the literal-minded Jake had replied.

"Their hawk."

The Eagles didn't have an eagle because eagles were endangered. But this year at least, the Murray High School Red Hawks had not only a human-sized hawk mascot but also a real live one. There had been an article about it in the paper Shane had seen last week.

It was a young hawk, almost recovered from a broken wing, nearly ready to be set free again. But in the meantime, some enterprising student had persuaded the wildlife service to let the school biology department care for it.

All of Murray was thrilled with their hawk. And the

high school football coach, no fool when it came to motivation, used it to great advantage. His team was going to give the hawk a great send-off at the end of the season. In the meantime, they were going to show the hawk their spirit.

"We'll steal the hawk," Shane had said, eyes alight with the prospect of the caper. "Steal their pride."

"Steal? We can't steal," Jake protested. "It's illegal."

Shane had given him a long-suffering look. "Not forever. Just for the week. Just so's they don't have him for the game. We'll put him back after. And—" he grinned "—in the meantime, we'll give them another mascot."

"What mascot?" Jake asked.

The grin spread all over Shane's face. "We'll give 'em a chicken."

Jake had gone along for moral support—and because he had a truck. But all the while he kept saying he wasn't sure about this.

What if they got caught?

"We won't get caught," Shane assured him. "You think they keep a guard at Murray High, for crying out loud?"

But they did have an overzealous history teacher. One who happened to be coming into the building to do a little late-night preparation just as Shane was sneaking out—with the hawk in a pillowcase under his arm.

There was a raft of potential charges: breaking and entering. Theft. Malicious mischief.

"The door wasn't locked," Shane protested.

But the cage had been.

"I didn't enter the cage!"

It didn't matter. The powers that were in Murray were

furious. The wildlife service was going to get him for endangering an avian predator.

"A what?" Shane had asked, mind reeling.

"A bird."

And that was before the two schools got into the act.

The principal of Murray High was rightly incensed that his school's integrity had been violated. It wasn't just the removal of the hawk, he said in measured, but censorious tones, it was its replacement. There was the small matter of the chicken. There were "implications...." He let the word trail off.

No one wondered what he meant.

The principal of Elmer High wasn't exactly thrilled, either. Shane's misguided larceny ("My *what?*" Shane had cried) reflected badly on the entire faculty and student body of Elmer High School, not to mention the town of Elmer itself.

The principal drew himself up to his full height and looked down his not inconsiderable nose at the miscreant before him. He was, he said, entirely in agreement with the principal of Murray that *something had to be done.*

The charges and possible consequences kept piling up.

Shane was over eighteen. Officially an adult. He could go to prison, he was informed. The hawk was valuable. It might even be a federal crime. A felony.

"You don't want a felony," Shane's court-appointed lawyer said quietly.

Shane, poleaxed by the whole thing, didn't say anything at all.

"Perhaps we can work out an alternative in a plea bargain," his lawyer said. "Judge Hamilton has been known to do some, shall we say, creative sentencing."

Enter Judge Hamilton.

And the chicken.

"You were trying to take away their pride," the judge had said, when all the powers had met and discussed and bargained, and Shane was brought into his chambers later that week.

He was articulating exactly what everyone else had wanted to call "larceny" or "theft" or "criminal mischief," and Shane, grateful at last to be understood—especially when it happened to be by the man who held his fate in his hands—nodded eagerly.

"You were going to take the hawk, leave them the chicken and bask in the glory of your cleverness, weren't you?"

Well, yes, he'd hoped to. But to say so seemed a little immodest. He didn't answer. But when he didn't, they all sat in silence—and probably would until doomsday—or until he admitted it. He nodded.

"You were maybe a little proud yourself?" the judge suggested. "Maybe a little...cocky?"

Shane shifted nervously at the judge's quiet, precise choice of words. He was fairly certain it hadn't been accidental.

"Perhaps it's *your* pride that needs a little pruning, Mr. Nichols," the judge went on. "And not Murray High School's."

The judge sentenced him to rent a chicken suit and appear in it at the Murray-Elmer game. He had to lead a cheer for Murray. He had to sit with the Murray cheerleaders.

Shane was aghast.

The judge wasn't through.

He had to attend the rest of Murray's home games that season. As a chicken.

It was an effective punishment. One that didn't end, as the judge had known it wouldn't, with the end of the games. There were plenty of scathing comments, behind-his-back and to-his-face chuckles, giggles and guffaws from both his own classmates and those at Murray.

But he endured it. Stoically. Stubbornly. He paid the price and never shirked it.

But it wasn't untrue to say he was desperate for the end of the season. As luck would have it, Murray had a good team that year, led by the best quarterback to come down the pike in a long, long time. His name was John Ransome Phillips, and he took them to the Montana state championship.

Murray supporters from miles around came to the game. And J.R. Phillips rose to the occasion.

He threw five touchdown passes that night. He ran the ball in for a sixth. Before the game was over, he had broken conference records for yardage and completions, cheered on by the entire student body, the whole town of Murray, the cheerleading squad, the Murray Red Hawk mascot—and a chicken.

When the game was over, Shane waited until the entire Murray football team had showered and dressed and left the locker room before he went in to change. It was bad enough enduring their comments during the game while he had his feathered suit on and his chicken head in place. At least he didn't have to listen to them while he got out of it.

But that night as he hurried to shed the miserable thing, the zipper stuck.

He got the head off. He got the feet off. But the damn bird body wouldn't budge. Feathers were jammed in the zipper's teeth. At least he guessed they were. He couldn't see it because it was against his back.

He fought with it. Cursed it. Yanked it. Contemplated ripping it.

He didn't, only because he'd paid a fifty-dollar deposit, and he still owed Mace half of the fifty. He had to get his deposit back, even if he had to drive all the way back to Elmer in the damned suit!

He was just contemplating the misery of walking across the parking lot in all his feathered splendor when the door to the locker room opened.

Murray's quarterback hero, dirty and sweaty and clearly as tired from local radio interviews and journalists' badgerings as from the football game, limped in. His brows lifted when he saw Shane.

Trapped in the chicken suit, Shane stiffened, steeling himself for the smart remark.

But Phillips just nodded. "Hey." And began to strip off his uniform shirt.

Shane, nonplussed, didn't move.

Phillips grabbed a towel and headed for the shower. "Need some help?"

"No!"

But he hadn't got it off by the time he heard Phillips flip-flopping his way back.

Shane shoved his feet into his boots, stuffed his clothes in the chicken head, tucked the fowl's floppy feet under his arm and headed out into the night.

There was no way on earth he was going to ask John Ransome Phillips, Murray High's greatest hero, to help him get out of his chicken suit!

Almost everyone else had gone home. There were only a few cars left in the lot. A few boys who'd driven over from the western Montana school were yelling at some Murray boys who weren't ready to go home.

Shane didn't have to walk anywhere near them. And if he'd been dressed in his jeans and jacket, no one would have noticed. Or cared.

But even in the dim light of the parking lot a six-foot chicken was, to put it bluntly, a sitting duck.

One of the western boys saw him, and suddenly they had something better to do than taunt the Murray boys.

"Let's get the chicken!"

Whooping and hollering, they surrounded him. There were three of them. One of Shane.

The punching started before half a dozen insults had been exchanged.

Shane fought hard, but the odds were bad. He was kicked and pounded. His nose was bloodied. His front tooth chipped. Then, in the midst of being ground into the dirt, he felt one of his attackers yanked off. Another was hauled away and punched hard.

By the time Shane scrambled up, fists flying, the outsiders had decided there was more valor in getting in their car and heading west than in pummeling the chicken.

Panting, bleeding, Shane stumbled around, trying to discover who his rescuer was.

J.R. Phillips.

The Murray quarterback was wiping blood off his own lip. His right eye was beginning to swell.

"Guess we showed them," J.R. Phillips said with a grin.

Shane swiped a hand across his mouth. He wobbled a bit, then steadied himself. "Guess so," he said, light-headed, wondering if he was imagining this.

J.R. Phillips had fought *for* him?

"You must like trouble," Phillips was saying, "walkin' around in that."

"No." Trouble, Shane was beginning to think, was highly over-rated.

"Why the hell you wearin' that damn suit then?"

"Zipper's stuck."

Phillips gave a bark of laughter. "And you couldn't ask me to undo it?" He paused, thought about it, then said, "No, I reckon you couldn't."

A moment of silent commiseration passed between them.

Then the quarterback stuck out his hand. "I'm Phillips. J.R. Phillips."

"I know," Shane said in a low voice. He took Phillips's hand. "Shane Nichols," he muttered.

Phillips looped an arm over Shane's shoulder and started to lead him back to the locker room. "My friends call me Rance."

Friends? Were they going to be friends? Shane wondered as he allowed himself to be led.

"You got guts, Shane Nichols. I'll say that," Rance told him. "You really got guts comin' here week after week dressed like that. Come on. Let's get you out of that thing."

"I owe you," Shane had said to him then.

He still did.

There wasn't a better man in the universe than Rance Phillips, and no one knew it better than Shane.

He wasn't some educated snob with a Harvard degree. He was a damn good bronc rider with a Harvard degree. He wasn't some snotty rancher's son who didn't know the first thing about earning a real living. He'd earned his own way since his father had cut him off when, determined to rodeo, Rance had decided to go down the road.

Shane knew he'd even gone to college on his rodeo money and hadn't given his father the satisfaction of sending him.

After Rance had graduated, Shane saw less of him. Sometimes Rance turned up at big rodeos. But eventually he didn't come at all.

Shane figured maybe he'd decided to go back to the ranch, settle down, make his peace with the old man. He hadn't known about Harvard Law.

But it wouldn't have mattered if he had.

What he did know was that Rance was a good man. A tough man. An educated man. And, doubtless now, a wealthy man.

But mostly, Shane knew, Rance was his own man.

The judge had done himself proud, whether Poppy wanted to admit it or not. He had found her the one man in the world worthy of her—and the only one that Shane would willingly step aside for.

But he couldn't pretend it didn't hurt.

The evening was bittersweet.

Shane sat through the meal—and it was the best one he could ever remember—thinking how much he could get used to living like this.

He liked the low, rambling ranch house. He liked its pine-paneled walls and comfortable leather chairs. He liked the stone fireplace and the Navajo rugs on the wide plank floors. He liked the dining room table that was cozy enough for the four of them, but which could expand to feed a branding crew. He liked it all, but mostly he liked the thought of having Poppy every night across the dinner table.

Every time he glanced her way, she smiled at him. Every time she spoke, she looked at him. Once her foot even connected with his ankle under the table. It might have been an accident, but it stayed, rubbing lightly and sending shivers of longing through him.

He struggled to keep his mind on the conversation. He made himself respond carefully and seriously to the questions Rance and the judge put to him. He found that all his study of Mace's herd gave him some ground for discussion. And his brother's concerns about water rights and grazing leases informed his opinions. He spoke for the small-scale rancher. Rance spoke for the large-scale one. The judge listened, gave his own opinions, asked questions.

He could never have imagined a time would come when he would be sitting at Judge Hamilton's table, making sensible conversation with the man.

Maybe he was growing up.

But it was too late.

He watched Rance charm Poppy without trying. He knew she intended to resist. It was what she'd wanted him here for, after all! But she couldn't. No one could.

It was just Rance's nature to be personable, to be handsome, to be low-key and a little off-the-wall. It was Rance's nature to make people feel comfortable with him. It wasn't Poppy's fault.

Shane didn't blame her.

He couldn't blame anyone. For once not even himself.

When the meal was over, she asked him to help her clear the table and he did.

He remembered the nights they had done dishes together in the cabin. At first they'd been awkward together. Then they had talked. Laughed. Learned. Loved.

He still loved her. Only tonight did he realize how much.

But he couldn't tell her.

Tonight Rance was here, helping too, while the judge went outside on the porch and smoked an after-dinner cigar.

So instead of talking to Poppy, he explained to Rance how he'd torn off his thumb. Then he heard about Rance's last ride, which had ended with him in the hospital with a badly broken arm.

"It made me stop and take stock," Rance said. "If I hadn't done it, I might still be goin' down the road. But it did, and I had to change my plans, play the new cards God dealt me."

A man who had Harvard as an option had pretty good cards, the way Shane saw it. His own deck seemed made up mainly of jokers. But he knew Rance wouldn't see that.

They talked about mutual friends, and Rance was surprised to hear Noah Tanner had moved into the valley.

"I've lost touch with so many rodeo people," he said ruefully. "It's what happens when you leave the circuit."

"You went on to bigger and better things," Shane pointed out.

But Rance shook his head. "Not better," he said firmly. "Just different. Here, let me help you with that," he said as Poppy struggled to carve the rest of the meat off the turkey. "I'm an old hand at this."

And while Shane watched, Rance did a creditable job of carving the rest of the bird. Was there anything Rance didn't do well?

When the judge came back in, he and Rance talked law. Then they talked about people Poppy knew, too, and then they talked about land development in the valley. Rance had definite ideas. So did the judge. So did Poppy.

She said something about some guy named Chad who had apparently been a not very scrupulous wheeler-dealer.

"Who's Chad?" Shane asked.

Poppy grimaced. "My ex-fiancé."

Shane hadn't even known she had an ex-fiancé. He felt sort of hollow, thinking about all the things he didn't know.

"Not the most scrupulous of men," her father elaborated. He had what Shane remembered as his "judge face" on. It had made him feel lower than the dirt on the bottom of a rock when he'd had it directed at him.

"What happened to him?"

"He plea bargained and left the state," Poppy said. The judge didn't say anything. His expression said it all.

Shane didn't say anything more, either. He sat back and listened. They continued to talk. Poppy smiled at him. He tried to smile back.

But the ache of knowing he was out of place was growing inside all the while, and there was no way to stop it. He knew he ought to get up and say thank you for the nice meal and leave them to it.

But he couldn't. Just a few minutes more, he told himself. A few minutes to pretend that this was his house, his life, his woman. Just a little while longer to sit and watch her, listen to her.

She was, he thought, the most beautiful, sensible, compassionate, intelligent woman in the world. She deserved a man with the same qualities she had.

She deserved Rance. Not him.

It was Rance who stretched and stood up first. "Reckon I'd better be going. I've got a client in Billings in the morning."

"I thought you were staying over tonight," the judge protested.

"Can't. I've got to be fresh bright and early." He

gave the judge a comradely smile. "You know how it goes. Gotta be on my toes."

Reluctantly the judge nodded and stood up, too. So did Poppy and Shane.

Rance tugged on his jacket, then crossed the room and took Poppy's hand in his. "Thank you. It was the best meal I've ever had."

Poppy gave him one of her megawatt smiles. "I'm glad you enjoyed it. I'm delighted you came."

"So am I. It was everything the judge promised it would be." There was a pause, and in the space of it his eyes had fastened on hers. And then Rance said, "So are you," and bent over her fingers and touched them with his lips.

Shane's teeth came together with a snap.

Rance glanced up and their eyes met. For a long moment, neither spoke. Then Shane broke off the gaze, stepped back.

But Rance reached out and cuffed Shane lightly on the arm. "Great to see you. I'll have to give Noah and Taggart a shout, and we can get together and do some more catching up."

Then, after shaking the judge's hand and promising to give him a call next week, Rance left.

"Guess I'd better be going, too," Shane said.

Poppy looked startled. "Are you sure? I mean, we barely had..." she colored, but forged on. "We haven't talked."

Shane couldn't talk. Couldn't say what he needed to say. He just had to do it. That's the sort of guy he was. He shook his head. "It's gettin' kind of late."

"He's right," said the judge.

For the first time tonight his gaze and Shane's locked.

It was just like it had been fourteen years ago: the judge and the troublemaker.

And the judge had won again.

Shane turned away. He looked at Poppy whose expression was uncertain. She gave him a tremulous smile.

He managed a tight one in return. "Thanks," he said. "I'll always remember this."

"We'll do it again," Poppy said quickly. "You can come and—"

"No. I can't."

"But—"

But Shane just shook his head.

"Good night, Nichols," the judge said. His voice was even, steady. There was no triumph in it. He was wholly matter-of-fact.

Of course he was. He was the law.

Shane was the outlaw.

Fine. So be it.

Shane was who he was. And because he was, he turned and did the last thing the judge wanted.

He took Poppy in his arms and kissed her, long and deep and hard.

It was everything he wanted, everything he'd ever hoped for, all he'd ever dreamed. And for this instant, it was his.

She was his.

But that was a dream. Reality was that he was a broken-down cowboy with no future and a muddy past, and she was a woman who deserved the best.

Shane tore himself away but couldn't avert his gaze. One last time he had to see her, to tell her with his eyes what his lips could never say.

I love you, he said to Poppy in his heart.

Eleven

Poppy didn't expect Shane would make love to her in the living room with her father looking on.

She did expect she would hear from him again.

But a day passed and then two. A week passed. He never called.

Her joy turned to worry. Her hopes turned to pain.

He loved her. She was sure of it. She'd seen it in his eyes. She'd felt it in his embrace. And that kiss…! She could still feel the urgency of his last kiss.

But she never heard from Shane.

She wondered if her father had sought him out and warned him off. He had, after all, had another man in mind for her. But she didn't really think so. The judge, for all his heavy-handed meddling, had never been one to discourage the friendship of anyone his daughter really liked.

Granted there was a little more than friendship involved here. But even so—and even if he didn't approve of Shane, which he never said he didn't—she didn't believe her father had done it.

If he had, she was sure Shane would have shown up just to defy him.

She debated calling his brother's house but decided against it. She had done the calling last time. She had invited him to dinner. Yes, he had come. But still, she didn't want to do all the running. The next move ought to be his.

What next move? A very good question.

She couldn't talk to her father about it. There was the matter of Rance, for one thing. But mostly there was the skeptical look he'd given her that night after Shane had left. And his words: "I hope you know what you're doing."

Then Poppy had said, "I do."

Now she wasn't so sure.

She couldn't talk to Milly, either. Milly was a nut case these days. She was obviously still in love with Cash but still equally humiliated by his having crashed her wedding.

"Would you rather I'd have let you marry the jerk?" Poppy had heard him yelling at Milly out in the greenhouse one afternoon.

"Maybe!" Milly had yelled back. "He couldn't possibly be a bigger jerk than you! There are no bigger jerks than you!"

Well, maybe there was one.

At least that's what Poppy was beginning to think. Had Shane just been toying with her? Leading her on? But then, how many guys drove clear back from Arizona to lead a girl on?

It didn't make any sense.

At least it didn't until the door opened to her shop late one Monday afternoon and Rance Phillips walked in.

At the sight of her, his lean face lit up with a grin. "Hey, I've been meaning to call you, but I've been running all over the damn state. That was a great dinner you cooked. It was a great evening all around."

At the time Poppy would have agreed with him. Now she managed a wan smile. "I enjoyed meeting you."

"I thought you wished me to hell and gone," Rance said frankly, propping himself against the cooler. "You looked like you had better things to do."

Poppy flushed and looked down at the snapdragons she was arranging. "My mistake," she said quietly.

Rance straightened up. "What do you mean? Did something happen?" The look he gave her was one of almost brotherly concern. "Shane isn't giving you trouble, is he?"

She shook her head. "No, he isn't giving me trouble! He isn't giving me anything! I haven't seen him since that night." Rance was the last person she ought to be laying this on, but she couldn't seem to stop herself.

Rance pushed away from the cooler and came to stand directly across the counter from her, placing his palms flat. "Tell me."

Poppy knew from the way he was standing that he wasn't going to move anytime soon. She imagined that this was the way he confronted a witness—with more or less gentleness.

It was very effective. She sighed. "There's nothing to tell. I thought we…Shane and I…were—" she shrugged "—you know…*were*. But apparently…I was wrong."

"Did he say so?"

"No. I told you. I haven't heard from him at all. He's

probably gone,'' she added, jamming the mutilated snap-
dragon into the bouquet.

Rance frowned. "Without telling you?"

"He never made me any promises."

"That kiss looked pretty promising."

"That's what I thought," she said sadly, and lifted
her shoulders. "And then I thought maybe my dad
scared him off."

"No. No way." Rance was positive about that.

"He didn't much like my father," Poppy said reflec-
tively. "Something to do with a prank he pulled when
he was a teenager, I guess. He never said why."

"No. He wouldn't." Rance smiled slightly. "It wasn't
one of his favorite memories."

"You know?"

Rance nodded.

"Tell me."

"Can't."

"But—"

"No. You ask him if you want to know."

"If I ever see him again." Poppy sighed and ran a
hand through her hair. "Probably I just expected too
much. It wasn't like we were a couple. Not really."

"Looked pretty much like a couple to me," Rance
said dryly.

"Yes, well, things got a little out of hand. We haven't
known each other long, really, but the time we spent
together was pretty special," she said wistfully. "I guess
I thought there was more to it than there really was. Or
maybe I just hoped."

"Based on the evidence, I'd say that was a reasonable
hope."

"Then why hasn't he called? Why hasn't he come
by?"

"Did he know your dad was bringing me home for dinner?"

"You mean, did he know about my dad's plans for me and you?"

Before she'd met him, she couldn't have imagined telling her father's choice such a thing. Now the words seemed to tumble out.

"Yeah," Rance said wryly, "those plans."

Poppy dipped her head. "That's...why I asked him to come."

"You didn't ask him to come because you loved him?"

Her cheeks burned. "No."

"I see." Rance looked thoughtful. Then he gave a small nod, touched her cheek with his finger, then tapped her on the end of her nose and headed toward the door.

"Can you ride?" the doctor echoed Shane's question and studied his determined patient over the top of his glasses. "Yes. Should you ride? Doubtful. Will that stop you?"

Together they said, "No."

"You could use a little more rehab," the doctor told him. "I wouldn't go back to the circuit just yet."

But Shane needed the distraction more than he needed the rehab. He needed a future to think about. Something to get his mind off the past.

"Got to," Shane said, leaning forward urgently as if he could exhort more enthusiasm from Doc Reeves if only he looked earnest enough.

"Broke?" the doctor asked with a wry smile. He'd patched his share of rough-stock riders over the years.

"Something like that." It wasn't his wallet. It was his heart.

He didn't know how else to deal with the loneliness. He'd never been lonely before in his life. The world had always seemed like one big party. Maybe it still was. He'd just lost his invitation.

He was doing the right thing, he assured himself. The only thing.

It had been a mistake, his getting to know her in the first place. She was out of his league, far too good for him. He'd always known that.

Their weekend together had been stolen from real life. It wasn't something to build on. Even though, for a few days, he'd tried to tell himself he could have forever— until her father had brought home Rance.

He couldn't compete with Rance.

He *wouldn't* compete with Rance.

But he couldn't stay around and watch, either. Elmer was too close. Even Montana wasn't big enough. He needed to get away, get moving, get on back down the road.

So he did.

Jenny thought he was crazy. Mace said, "You sure about this?"

Shane was sure he had no future here. That was enough.

He thanked the doctor, tugged down his hat and went in search of a rodeo.

He drew a nasty little spinning bull called Frogger's Revenge.

Shane had ridden him once before at the Cow Palace in San Francisco. He'd been stomped once, too, in New Mexico somewhere.

Good, he told himself. It would be a challenge. He needed a challenge. His thumb was stiff. He'd been flexing it on and off all during the drive to the small town rodeo in eastern Washington.

He got to the rodeo grounds not long before the bull riding began, left his truck near the concession stand and carried his rigging bag behind the chutes. He picked up his contestant's number from the secretary and got her to stick it on the back of his shirt.

She looked delighted to see him. "Shane, how are you? I heard about your accident. This your first ride after?"

He nodded. "Couldn't hardly wait to get back." He thought his voice sounded a little hollow. But he felt the adrenaline begin to pick up and he drew a deep breath and looked around, absorbing the sights, the smells, the sounds he'd missed.

She patted his back, then gave him a peck on the cheek. "Good luck."

He winked at her. "Here's hopin' I won't need it."

"Hey, Shane!" A couple of cowboys gave him a wave. Two more looked over from where they stood on the chutes, already preparing. "How ya doin'?"

"Good," Shane said. "Good." He pulled out his bull rope and hung it on the fence, then got out his rosin. *Good.* But he would be better when he'd finished his ride, when he was fully and completely involved again, when every other thought that raced through his brain wasn't about Poppy.

He was up fourth. And when he scrambled up to put his rope on the bull, habit and instinct began to take over. He pulled the rope up tight, then tighter. He flexed his thumb a few times and prayed it was ready. Then he pulled the glove on his riding hand and settled onto the back of the bull, inching up into the rope, knees in, toes out, shoulders square.

Just like old times.

He nodded his head. "Let's go."

The chute gate swung open. The bull blew out, spun, dipped, kicked, thrust, spun again.

Shane clung. Focused. Shifted. Dipped. The arena whirled around him as if he were the eye and it was the hurricane. The cheering crowd was a blur of faces—except one.

Right at the buzzer when his strength, try and balance all gave out and he went flying, his only thought was: *What the hell was Rance doing there?*

Because sure as shootin', that was Rance standing there by the announcer's booth, grinning his head off. Shane scrambled to his feet and sprinted to the fence.

But self-preservation was purely instinct at this point. His mind was on Rance. Wasn't having the girl and the law degree and the future enough for him? Was he still hankering after a gold buckle, too?

Shane didn't know. He wasn't going to ask. Rance might be his buddy, but there was just so much good luck a guy could watch.

"Good job, Shane!" One of the bull riders clapped his on the back.

"Seventy-eight! Not a bad way to come back," another said.

"Yeah," Shane muttered. He stuffed his rope in his rigging bag and headed toward his truck.

"Shane! Hey! Shane Nichols!"

He knew who was yelling. For a moment he didn't even turn. But he could hear the footsteps running after him, and he knew there was no avoiding it. Finally he turned around.

He didn't smile. So what if it made him a poor sport. It was just one more tick against his name at the final accounting. One more in a misspent life like his shouldn't make a helluva lot of difference.

"Rance." It was acknowledgment, no more.

"Shane." Rance hesitated, the first time Shane had seen him at a loss. Then he said, "Good ride. How'd the thumb hold up?"

Shane hadn't even noticed. He wiggled it. It was still there. It hurt. Throbbed really. "It's all right. What're you doin' here?"

Rance smiled a little wistfully. "Well, I wish I could say I'd come out of retirement, but—"

"Want to win a buckle to go with everything else you've got?" The words were out of his mouth before he could stop himself. Why in God's name didn't he shut up? He didn't mean to sound bitter. He didn't *want* to be spiteful and small.

"If I thought I could, I might come back." Rance took the question at face value. Then he shook his head. "But it isn't gonna happen."

"Then why are you here?"

"You mean, why aren't I home with Poppy?"

Damn it. How like Rance not to pull any punches. It was what Shane always respected about him—that he never hesitated to say exactly what needed to be said.

But damn him for saying it now, for rubbing it in.

But at the same time, Shane knew it served him right. And there was going to be no peace in his life until he accepted it.

"Yes." He tried to sound indifferent. It was hard when the word hissed out between his teeth.

Rance nodded, smiling slightly as he shook his head. "I thought that's what you meant. I was afraid of that. It's exactly the sort of thing you would think. Damn it, man, Poppy doesn't want anything to do with me. She wants you!"

"That's crazy."

Rance grinned. "Yeah, it is. But, hey, there's no accounting for taste."

Shane gritted his teeth. "It isn't a joke."

Rance sobered at once. "No, it's not. It's the absolute bedrock truth, buddy. She's sitting back there in Livingston crying her eyes out over a sorry sucker like you." He fixed Shane in his pale blue gaze. "And you're out here howling at the moon without her."

Shane stared at him. "That's bull," he said, but he couldn't help the surge of hope bursting in him. God, he wished it were true!

Rance just looked at him pityingly. "Right," Rance said. "It's bull." And he turned on his boot heel and started to walk away.

"Wait a minute! Wait just a damn minute!" Shane took three quick strides and grabbed Rance's arm.

Rance stopped. He waited. He looked at Shane. Didn't speak. Just stood there.

Shane opened his mouth. The words wouldn't come out. He shook his head. "She wasn't crying?" he said urgently. God, he didn't want her crying, but—!

Rance's mouth twisted. "Poetic license. No, she wasn't crying. Not literally. Not on the outside, anyway. But on the inside, yeah, man, she is."

Shane denied it. "Somethin' else upset her, then. It doesn't have anything to do with me."

Rance rolled his eyes. "When'd you get so good at lying to yourself? It has everything to do with you, Shane. She told me."

Shane's eyes bugged. "She *told* you? You *talked* about me. To her?"

"Why not? You're my friend. She's your girl."

"She's *not!*"

Rance made a sound suspiciously like a groan. "Fine, she's not." He turned away again.

Shane yanked him back. "What'd she say?"

"Ask her."

"She's not here." He looked quickly, nervously around. "Is she?"

"No, she's not. She's back home lonely as hell, thanks to you. What was it, some latent streak of cussed nobility that made you take off like that?"

Shane didn't answer.

"That was it, wasn't it?" Rance peered at him closely. "Step aside for the better man?" he said mockingly.

Shane's jaw bunched. He scowled. "Something like that." He didn't need Rance making a joke out of it.

But Rance just said mildly, "Well, thank you. You're mistaken, though. I'm not the better man."

"The star quarterback? The National Merit scholar. The heir to the Phillips's ranch? The Phi Beta Kappan? The guy with the Harvard law degree?"

"They're okay." Rance dug a toe of his boot in the dirt. "But they're not..." He lifted his gaze and met Shane's. "I looked up to you."

"*Me?* Oh sure. You wanted to grow up and wear a chicken suit maybe?" Shane's voice was scathing. "Or get your ass hauled to jail for malicious mischief? Or maybe you wanted to go off so half-cocked you stole the wrong woman from the wedding!"

"*What?*"

"Never mind. Looked up to me? You're outa your mind!"

"No," Rance said stubbornly. "I'm not. I'm tellin'

you, all those other things came easy. The quarterback-ing. The grades. All of it—but the bronc riding and turn-ing my back on my dad's ultimatums. I never took any risks until then. You took risks all the time. They didn't always turn out the way you wanted them to—" Rance grinned faintly "—like the chicken. But you had guts. And you lived with the consequences. You taught me a lot, Nichols." His voice went quiet. "You were my hero."

Poleaxed, Shane simply stared. "That doesn't make sense." It didn't. It was completely ridiculous. Him? A *hero*? To *Rance*? "Gimme a break."

"I'm trying to. I'm trying to tell you that you're blowing it. Poppy wants you. She's waiting for you. But she's not gonna wait forever. What the hell do you think I'm doing here? I called your brother, badgered your sister-in-law, bugged your doctor, pestered 'em down at the PRCA. Drove everybody nuts looking for you. And when you finally called home and said you were riding here, I thought, hell, what's a nine-hundred-mile drive if it'll keep my buddy from screwing up his life. So—" he spread his hands "—here I am."

Shane swallowed. "You're...serious." It started as a question, but by the time he got the word out, he knew the answer.

"You could say that," Rance drawled. "The rest, ol' buddy, is up to you."

It seemed simple.

He got in his truck. Filled it with gas. Headed north-east. Drove straight through.

He was in Livingston the next day. Parked right down the street from Poppy's Garden.

Then he sat in his truck and didn't move. *Couldn't* move.

Because all of a sudden it wasn't so simple.

Maybe it had never been that simple. Because suddenly it wasn't just needing Rance to back away, to give him his blessing. It had just been easier to believe that. Easier than believing that the problem wasn't out there.

It was inside. In him.

Shane sat there in his truck and thought about turning up out of the blue and walking into Poppy's life again, expecting her to be glad to see him. Hoping she loved him the way he loved her.

And he thought about how ridiculous that was.

He might love her. She might even think she loved him. But then what? What on earth did he have to offer a woman like her?

Poppy had intelligence, a good education, a job she'd built up from scratch and had made a success of.

He had none of the above.

He was bright enough—in what his sister-in-law called a "gut instinct sort of way." But his education had been the school of hard knocks, his job was about to become a thing of the past. And he'd only made a middling success of that.

He'd hoped—and worked—for an NFR gold buckle. He'd given it his all. His all hadn't been enough.

He'd won $271 at the rodeo yesterday. He'd almost got his head kicked in. Muscles he'd forgotten he had were aching now like they hadn't ached in years. His thumb had survived, but he couldn't grip the steering wheel all the way home.

There weren't going to be many more bull rides in his future, and he knew it. There might not be any. There wasn't a lot of sense in going out and taking the risk of riding a ton of bovine ferocity if you didn't think you had a shot at winning the world.

Shane knew now he didn't have a chance of winning the world.

He knew, too, what he did have: nothing.

No prospects. No plans. No hopes.

Unless you wanted to count the hope that Poppy loved him.

It seemed too much to ask for.

And even if she did, he had no big history of success. He couldn't even steal a damn hawk and do it right. It would be worse—the worst thing he could imagine—to fail her.

"Shane?" Jenny's voice came through the barely open bedroom door.

He debated pretending he was asleep. He'd come back to Mace's, managed a few polite mumbles, declined Jenny's offer of dinner, then had taken refuge in the spare bedroom. He told them he was tired. He said he'd driven straight through and he needed sleep.

He didn't say there was a pain so deep in his gut and his heart that he didn't imagine it would ever go away.

If his brother saw something was wrong, he would have the good sense not to say it. Jenny was a different matter. She would sympathize. She would commiserate. She would care. That was the last thing he needed tonight.

So he held perfectly still and breathed as slowly and deeply as his ribs, still sore from the bull riding, would allow.

"Telephone." Jenny pushed the door open wider. "For you. It sounds important."

There was nobody on earth he wanted to talk to now. Unless—

He sat bolt upright. Poppy?

Jenny came in and handed him the portable, then left again.

He swallowed, licked his lips, then pressed the receiver against his ear. "H'lo?"

"Nichols?"

It wasn't Poppy. But he would have known that stern, gravelly voice anywhere. "I saw you sitting in your truck outside my daughter's shop this afternoon."

Shane shut his eyes. Even in the darkness, he couldn't face this. He couldn't listen. Couldn't tolerate hearing the old man tell him what he already knew too damn well: that he was a loser, that he'd already lost.

"Why'd you leave?"

The question was so totally unexpected that when Shane opened his mouth, he found no words. Only air.

For a moment he groped for an answer, then gave the only one he had. "You know why," he said on an angry, harsh breath. "You, of all people, know that."

"No, I don't." The judge's voice was firm, implacable. "I thought you loved her." Again he left Shane open-mouthed. "Don't you?"

Guilty? Or innocent?

Guilty. As always. "Yes." Shane said hoarsely.

"Then why did you leave?"

"Because I— There's no point. I have nothing to offer her, and you know it. You know what I'm like!"

In the silence he heard the judge take a long slow breath. Then, "I thought I did," Judge Hamilton said quietly. "I thought you had the courage of your convictions. A long time ago I thought you were rough edged and cocky as hell. But I was sure you had enough intestinal fortitude to take a punishment I'd never have dared give a lesser man. You did. And I respected you for it.''

He paused a moment and let that astonishing notion sink in. Like Rance's looking up to him, it was going to take some getting used to.

"I'll tell you one thing I never thought until today, Shane Nichols," the judge went on. "I never thought you were a chicken."

He was a chicken.

Poppy had seen his truck out in front of her shop this afternoon. She'd been helping a customer choose a wedding anniversary bouquet, and out of the corner of her eye, she'd spied a red truck through the glass. Her stomach had somersaulted, her mind had spun, her heart had begun thumping to beat the band, and she'd started grinning like a fool.

"Yes, being married for fifty-three years in this day and age is pretty amazing, isn't it?" the woman ordering the bouquet had said, evidently thinking that Poppy's sudden smile was a reaction to her last remark.

It was, Poppy had agreed. Almost as amazing as the fact that Shane had come back to her.

She watched. She waited. She barely paid attention to another word the woman said. Her attention was totally caught by the red truck parked across the street.

And then, just as she'd finished writing down the order, she looked up and saw him drive away.

At first she hadn't believed it. She'd thought he was moving his truck or going around the block or...or...something. Anything other than what eventually she came to realize he'd done.

He'd left.

And he never came back.

"That was Shane? Wasn't that Shane?" she'd demanded a few minutes later, after her customer left and her father came into her shop.

The judge hesitated for a moment, then gave a small shrug.

"It was," Poppy said, angry and aching at the same time. "I'm sure it was. I thought he'd come back to me." Her throat felt tight and she couldn't get any more words past the lump in it. This was worse than when her mother had died.

Then it was awful, but it was over. Then she'd been empty, but she'd waited and worked and prayed and hoped—and gradually, slowly, she'd got her life back. There had been a definite bottom. And there was the slow, hard way back up.

But at least she'd known when she'd hit bottom.

With Shane she was never sure.

He'd come to dinner. She'd hoped. He'd kissed her. She'd dreamed. He'd left. And still she'd hoped—for a time.

And then she'd felt empty. And aching. And lost. She'd thought it was the bottom. She'd been learning to live with it, to be patient with it, to hope that it would get better.

And then when she'd seen his truck—for an instant all her hopes and dreams came flooding back.

Only to be dashed again.

The glass wasn't simply empty this time. She felt as if Shane had broken it right in front of her.

"He's a good man," her father said quietly.

Poppy stared. "I'm sure he'd be surprised to hear you say that."

"Do you think so?" The judge looked thoughtful.

"*I'm* surprised," she said, which was only the truth.

And she wasn't sure she agreed with him, either. "He's a stubborn, hardheaded, impulsive, no-good jerk."

Her father smiled and leaned in to give her a kiss. "Just in case...hold that thought."

Whatever that meant, Poppy thought irritably now, as she stared at the ceiling in her bedroom and wished she could fall asleep. She remembered, after her mother had died, that sleep was the one thing that helped. She'd needed a lot of it then. She thought she could use a good eight hours now.

But she'd been lying here forever, and she was no nearer sleep than she had been when she went to bed. And that had been how long ago? She glanced at the clock on her bedside table.

Only an hour?

Well, it felt like forever. At this rate the night would take five years to pass.

"Damn him," she muttered. "Oh, damn him." She rolled over and punched her pillow. Wally, who had been sleeping at the foot of the bed, stirred, lifted his head and gave her a look of feline disapproval.

"He's a jerk," Poppy told him.

Wally yawned and put his head back down and began once more to snore.

The sudden sound of knocking on her front door caused her to jump. Who on earth?

Probably someone who left the tavern down the street early and decided to raise a little cain on his way home. She ignored it.

The knocking came again. More insistently.

Poppy got up and tugged on her robe, then padded to peer out past the curtain in her living room window, which gave her a view of whoever might be standing on her second-floor porch.

He had his back to her and stood with his shoulders

hunched in the snow that had been coming down since early evening. But there was no question who it was.

Poppy shivered, dropped the curtain, went back to the bedroom and crawled back into bed. She had no desire at all to talk to Shane Nichols.

If he'd had anything she wanted to hear, he could have said it this afternoon. If he was here now, it was because her father had called him, had *made* him come. And to say what?

She didn't want to know.

He knocked again. Louder this time.

Poppy pulled the pillow over her head. "Go away."

More pounding. "Poppy! Open up. Come on, Poppy! Open the door!" He was making more noise now than the drunks who came out of the bar down the street. At the rate he was going, he'd wake old Mrs. Patters in the apartment in the next building, and she'd call the police.

"Good," Poppy muttered. "I hope she does." It would be fitting. She would love to see him hauled away.

"Poppy!" More hammering. "I want to talk to you! I *need* to talk to you!"

"You had your chance," Poppy said into the pillow. She pulled the covers over her head.

"Poppy!"

She ignored him.

Mrs. Patters didn't. The window in the apartment next door scraped up. "Are you drunk, young man? Go home! Go home right now or I'll call the police!" The window banged down again.

There was silence.

Then there was a quieter tapping sound. "Poppy?" muffled. "Poppy. Open up." Then, "Oh, hell, if that's the way you're going to be...."

And as she lifted the pillow, Poppy heard the sound of footsteps going back down the wooden stairs.

She slumped face down on the bed and felt shudders run through her. He was gone. It was the right thing to have done. He was gone. Good. He was gone. It was for the best. But she felt hollow, desperate, aching.

She heard a scraping and a scrabbling sound outside her bedroom window. She stopped cold. Didn't move.

There came an indistinct, irritated mutter, then more scraping and the sound of metal creaking. Then there was a sharp rap on her window.

"You want me to kill myself? Fine, you'll get your wish. If you don't open this damn window in five seconds, my thumb will fall off, I'll lose my grip and land on my head!"

She flew out of bed and yanked back the curtains. Shane was hanging on to the ladder of her ice-and snow-covered fire escape. He grinned at her.

She flung open the window. "You idiot! What do you think you're doing?"

"You could've opened the door," he said with maddening logic. "But I suppose you were trying to say you were ticked at me."

"I *am* mad at you!"

"Don't blame you," he said matter-of-factly. "Could we, um, maybe...talk about that? Inside," he added. "I really am losin' my grip."

Poppy made an inarticulate mutter and reached out a hand to haul him in. He heaved himself up the rest of the way and clambered through the open window, then stood in the middle of her bedroom and shook the snow off like a wet dog.

"Shane!"

He grinned. "Poppy!" And he reached for her.

She evaded him. "No. I'm not kissing you. I'm not!"

The light went out of his eyes. The smile faded from his face. He jammed his hands in his jeans pockets. ''I don't blame you for that, either.'' He ducked his head and ran his tongue over his lips.

Poppy grabbed her robe and pulled it on. She turned on the light and then wrapped her arms across her chest, as if a bright light and thin arms could protect her.

Shane lifted his gaze once more and met hers. ''I love you,'' he said.

Just like that.

Just like that he cut right through all her defenses. Smashed them. Crumbled them. Left her speechless. And still afraid. She didn't say a word. *Couldn't* have if her life had depended on it. She just looked at him, hope warring with doubt in her eyes.

He gave her a faint smile as if he understood all too well.

''I do,'' he said. ''I don't deserve you. And I don't have a damn thing to offer you. But I have to say it. Your father was right. I couldn't—'' his mouth twisted ''—be a chicken about it, even if I wanted to.''

''My father?'' So this *was* at his instigation? She backed away, as if distance could help.

But nothing was going to help. She ought to have known that by now.

''He called me,'' Shane said. ''He said he saw me today outside your shop. He asked me why I didn't go in. But he knew why.''

''Why?'' Poppy found herself whispering.

''Because I was afraid. And I was proud. They don't make a good combination. I'd taken a good hard look at all you had to offer and all I did, and the scales were nowhere near even. I didn't want to come to you that way.''

''But—''

"He knew it. He knows a lot about my pride," Shane said quietly. "Someday, if we have a someday," he added, "I'll tell you about it. About the chicken."

"The chicken?" Poppy said, mystified.

Shane was sure she would appreciate the chicken. "He made me start thinking," he went on doggedly. "And remembering. I remembered what you said. It was like you said about when your mother died. I'm facing my future, and frankly, it looks damned empty. I don't know what I'm going to do. I have to figure that out. In the meantime, I've got to begin to put into it the things that will give it some meaning. And I will," he said firmly. "But I don't want to start with things, Poppy. I want to start with you."

Poppy just stared at him mutely. And then she felt as if a band that had been constricting her chest, impeding her breathing, choking her very life away, had suddenly loosed. She shuddered. She trembled. She started to cry.

"Oh, hell," Shane muttered. "Don't. God, please, don't! I'll go. I'm sorry." He was backing toward the window even as he spoke.

"No!" Poppy flung herself at him. He stumbled back, and she grabbed him, slid her arms inside his jacket and buried herself against him, hanging on for dear life.

"Oh, wow," she heard Shane mumble. "Oh, wow. Does this mean—?" He held her out from him and looked into her face.

She gave him a watery smile and a gurgling laugh, and he grinned from ear to ear.

"I guess it does," he said. Then he wrapped his arms and toppled them both onto her bed.

Wally hissed, then huffed and hopped off the bed.

"Sorry," Shane said to his twitching tail as the cat stalked out of the room. But then he shook his head. "No, I'm not," he corrected and smiled down at Poppy once more. "Not sorry at all. This is something I'm never gonna regret. Never in a million years."

He loved her then.

He loved her with all the gentleness and care and consideration of which he was capable. He loved her with all the passion and desire and need that had been building in him since he'd loved her last.

And the miracle was she loved him, too.

Not just with words, though she gave him those, but beyond words. He could see it in her eyes when she looked at him. He could hear it in her voice no matter what she said. He could feel it in the way she touched him.

God, the way she touched him! For all the pleasure he tried to give her, she repaid him a hundredfold.

"Where did you learn to do that?" he asked her toward morning when he was lying there weak as a rag from the loving they'd shared.

Poppy smiled down at him and ran a finger down the center of his chest and stomach. All the way down. "I had a lot of time while you were running around the country to think of what I'd like to do to you."

Shane shivered. His toes clenched. He couldn't believe that after all they'd already done tonight that she could still arouse him, but she definitely could. "You're welcome to do that anytime," he told her. "Anytime at all."

It was getting light before Poppy fell asleep in his arms.

Shane was tired, too. He still hadn't slept since the day before yesterday, and though there was a lot to be said for adrenaline, even that had its limits. But he couldn't close his eyes. He had to keep watching her, to be sure she was really there in his arms.

He turned his head and pressed a kiss to her cheek, and she opened her eyes.

"It's not a dream?" she said sleepily, and touched his face with her hand.

He shook his head. "I hope not." He rolled onto his side, facing her. "I want it to be forever. Will you marry me? I know Rance is the better bet," he went on quickly without giving her a chance to answer.

"Yes."

"I know he has more to offer. Hey!" He scowled. "You aren't supposed to agree with me!"

Poppy laughed. "That was *yes* to your proposal, my love." She pushed him back against the sheet, then slid on top of him, moving sinuously and sending shudders of desire straight through him. "Of course," she said thoughtfully, "Rance is a brilliant man. A handsome man. A clever man. A good man."

"Enough!"

Poppy fitted their bodies together. "But he's not the right man—for me."

"Thank God," Shane muttered. And he began to move once more.

They were married in the springtime.

In the church where Milly hadn't married Mike, in the church where Cash had got his face slapped and Poppy had once upon a time been kidnapped from.

It was a beautiful wedding. Poppy did the flowers herself. Milly and Cash were both in the wedding party, and while they didn't exactly smile at each other, they didn't come to blows, either. Rance showed up with a girl no one had ever seen before, and if he didn't introduce her, Shane and Poppy didn't care.

Poppy's father walked her down the aisle and looked

surprisingly pleased as he gave her, with his blessing, to the white-faced groom who waited for her.

Afterward, they had a reception at Huggins's. Poppy and Shane agreed on almost all of the details for the sit-down dinner. Poppy wanted to be a little more conservative in terms of cost. Shane, as usual, threw caution to the winds.

Poppy gave in. They were only getting married once, after all. Their guests—all two hundred and fifty of them—had prime rib and Huggins's special potatoes along with salad and huge bowls of fruit. They cut a scrumptious three-layer wedding cake afterward.

The whole day was wonderful, and everyone knew it. Especially the bride and groom.

"I told you so," Shane said in Poppy's ear after he'd fed her a bite of cake and taken a bite from her fingers in return.

"You did. It was perfect," Poppy agreed and kissed him on the mouth. Then she smiled impishly. "And you were absolutely right. The prime rib was wonderful. Much better than having chicken."

*   *   *   *   *

Does Cash ever win Milly back? Find out in Anne McAllister's next Code of the West book, THE COWBOY CRASHES A WEDDING, *coming July 1998—only from Silhouette Desire!*

Take 4 bestselling love stories FREE

Plus get a FREE surprise gift!

Special Limited-time Offer

Mail to Silhouette Reader Service™

3010 Walden Avenue
P.O. Box 1867
Buffalo, N.Y. 14240-1867

YES! Please send me 4 free Silhouette Desire® novels and my free surprise gift. Then send me 6 brand-new novels every month, which I will receive months before they appear in bookstores. Bill me at the low price of $2.90 each plus 25¢ delivery and applicable sales tax, if any.* That's the complete price and a savings of over 10% off the cover prices—quite a bargain! I understand that accepting the books and gift places me under no obligation ever to buy any books. I can always return a shipment and cancel at any time. Even if I never buy another book from Silhouette, the 4 free books and the surprise gift are mine to keep forever.

225 BPA A3UU

Name	(PLEASE PRINT)	
Address	Apt. No.	
City	State	Zip

This offer is limited to one order per household and not valid to present Silhouette Desire® subscribers. *Terms and prices are subject to change without notice.
Sales tax applicable in N.Y.

UDES-696

©1990 Harlequin Enterprises Limited

As seen on TV!
Free Gift Offer

With a Free Gift proof-of-purchase from any Silhouette® book,
you can receive a beautiful cubic zirconia pendant.

This gorgeous marquise-shaped stone is a genuine cubic
zirconia—accented by an 18" gold tone necklace.

(Approximate retail value $19.95)

Send for yours today...
compliments of ▼ *Silhouette*®

To receive your free gift, a cubic zirconia pendant, send us one original proof-of-
purchase, photocopies not accepted, from the back of any Silhouette Romance™,
Silhouette Desire®, Silhouette Special Edition®, Silhouette Intimate Moments®
or Silhouette Yours Truly™ title available at your favorite retail outlet, together with
the Free Gift Certificate, plus a check or money order for $1.65 U.S./$2.15 CAN. (do
not send cash) to cover postage and handling, payable to Silhouette Free Gift Offer. We
will send you the specified gift. Allow 6 to 8 weeks for delivery. Offer good until
March 31, 1998, or while quantities last. Offer valid in the U.S. and Canada only.

Free Gift Certificate

Name: _____

Address: _____

City: _____ State/Province: _____ Zip/Postal Code: _____

Mail this certificate, one proof-of-purchase and a check or money order for postage
and handling to: SILHOUETTE FREE GIFT OFFER 1998. In the U.S.: 3010 Walden
Avenue, P.O. Box 9077, Buffalo, NY 14269-9077. In Canada: P.O. Box 613, Fort Erie,
Ontario L2Z 5X3.

FREE GIFT OFFER   084-KFD
ONE PROOF-OF-PURCHASE
To collect your fabulous FREE GIFT, a cubic zirconia pendant, you must include this
original proof-of-purchase for each gift with the properly completed Free Gift Certificate.

084-KFDR2

SILHOUETTE WOMEN KNOW ROMANCE WHEN THEY SEE IT.

And they'll see it on **ROMANCE CLASSICS**, the new 24-hour TV channel devoted to romantic movies and original programs like the special **Romantically Speaking—Harlequin™ Goes Prime Time.**

Romantically Speaking—Harlequin™ Goes Prime Time introduces you to many of your favorite romance authors in a program developed exclusively for Harlequin® and Silhouette® readers.

Watch for **Romantically Speaking—Harlequin™ Goes Prime Time** beginning in the summer of 1997.

If you're not receiving ROMANCE CLASSICS, call your local cable operator or satellite provider and ask for it today!

Escape to the network of your dreams.

See Ingrid Bergman and Gregory Peck in *Spellbound* on Romance Classics.

FIVE STARS
MEAN SUCCESS

If you see the "5 Star Club" flash on a book,
it means we're introducing you to one of our
most STELLAR authors!

Every one of our Harlequin and Silhouette
authors who has sold over 5 MILLION BOOKS
has been selected for our "5 Star Club."

We've created the club so you won't miss
any of our bestsellers. So, each month
we'll be highlighting every original book within
Harlequin and Silhouette written by our
bestselling authors.

NOW THERE'S NO WAY ON EARTH OUR
STARS WON'T BE SEEN!

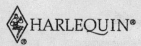 

P5STAR

Available in February 1998

ANN MAJOR

CHILDREN OF DESTINY
When Passion and Fate Intertwine...

SECRET CHILD

Although everyone told Jack West that his wife,
Chantal — the woman who'd betrayed him and sent
him to prison for a crime he didn't commit — had
died, Jack knew she'd merely transformed herself
into supermodel Mischief Jones. But when he
finally captured the woman he'd been hunting,
she denied everything. Who was she really —
an angel or a cunningly brilliant counterfeit?"

"Want it all? Read Ann Major."
—**Nora Roberts,** *New York Times*
bestselling author

Don't miss this compelling story
available at your favorite retail outlet.
Only from Silhouette books.

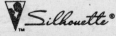